ULTIMATE
LESBIAN

ULTIMATE
LESBIAN EROTICA
EDITED BY NICOLE FOSTER

2007

alyson books
NEW YORK

This trade paperback original is published by
Alyson Books
P.O. Box 1253
Old Chelsea Station
New York, New York 10113-1251

Distribution in the United Kingdom by
Turnaround Publisher Services Ltd.
Unit 3, Olympia Trading Estate
Coburg Road, Wood Green
London N22 6TZ United Kingdom

First edition: January 2007
07 08 09 10 11 **a** 10 9 8 7 6 5 4 3 2 1
ISBN 1-55583-970-3
ISBN-13 978-1-55583-970-3

Library of Congress Cataloging-in-Publication Data is on file.

Book design by Victor Mingovits.

CONTENTS

INTRODUCTION

SITTING BEFORE MOUNDS (AHEM) of lesbian erotica submissions, I was like a kid in a candy store—somewhat daunted by the choices I would have to make but thrilled by the potential rewards.

I had some tough decisions to make. I had to ask, which authors had taken me the farthest, which stories were sure to push *you* over the edge? It was hard work; I toiled day and night. But dear reader, as I know you know, I would do anything for you and I hope you feel my efforts were worth it.

Ultimately (that's right), there's a little something

for everyone: hot dripping candles, a straight girl's first threeway with two women, drag kings getting it on, spanking, foot fetishes, phone sex, voyeurism, and lots and lots of exhibitionism (on a cruise ship, at the gym, and even in Amsterdam's Red Light District). A story not to miss is the very last one: a writer has an orgy with mischievous ghosts who are under the instruction of her dearly departed girlfriend's spirit.

A very special thank you to the always-original, always-inventive writers published here. You inspire us to live out our fantasies...And to our faithful readers who, in the end, are the ultimate arbiters of what's hot. This is all for you.

And now I'm off to do a little further research on hot wax play...

Enjoy!
Nicole Foster

LICK 'ER LICENSE

SHANEL ODUM

I GRAB THE FROSTED bottle from the crowded shelf behind me and pour a steady stream of Absolut Citron into the ice-filled, tin shaker with exaggerated flair. In a single sweeping gesture, I garnish the chilled martini glass with a lime wedge and strain the pink cocktail with practiced precision. No matter how many times I repeat the carefully choreographed routine, I can't help but swallow a satisfied grin as the last drop trickles into the glass, gently kissing the rim. The girls know they can always count on this bartender to quench their thirst.

The club is throbbing. It's one in the morning and

the party is reaching its climax. The reggaeton bassline erupts from the massive speakers while the strobe lights slice through artificial fog with a pulsing rhythm that echoes the DJ's renderings. The sweat-slick dance floor is swelling with drenched, half-naked bodies, and the Friday night partygoers are still pouring in.

The club may not have an official dress code but the young lesbian community seems to follow an implicit one. Butches and bois sport their usual weekend uniforms—white wife-beater or jersey, durag and baseball cap, jeans and sneaks. The ones with a little more dip in their swagger wouldn't be caught out there without a rubber hard-on nestled in the fold of their boxer briefs. The girly girls wear everything from curve-clinging hip huggers to micro minis, but seem to adhere to the basic essentials of femme wear—stilettos, cleavage, and a glossy pout.

All my regulars are here. I'll be the first to admit that my vice has taken its toll on my memory, so it's easier to remember my customers by the drinks they order. There's Henney (straight up)—kind of a gruff-voiced ball player, who always sports a perfectly gel slicked ponytail. She swims in her oversized Sean Johns and camouflages her C-cups with the same sports bra she wore as a high school point guard. Her sexuality is claustrophobic—she wouldn't dare attempt to lock it in anybody's closet. Every week she parades her porn-star girlfriend, Midori (sour), around the bar with an ironclad grip and a watchful eye. Tonight, the XXX actress is perched on five-inch daggers, habitually flicking her pierced tongue like a python, and wearing the brand new gold sequin J-Lo dress Henney bought from Dr. J's for her earlier that day.

And of course there's OO7, the veteran, crew cut lesbian who manages to slither her way into every girl party in New York City. You'll never catch her prowling without her shades and the only girls she manages to conquer are *carne fresca.*

Fresh meat. These are the bicurious or recently pledged lesbabies craving mentorship amongst their new sorority sisters. These are the chicks that flash their older sisters' ID for admittance into our weekly carnal celebration. They roam in packs, cloaked in their newfound gayness, always overly adorned with rainbow accessories.

Tossing her weave over her glazed, bronze shoulders, Red Devil saunters over to my bar for a quick drink between sets. Her body glitter winks under the glare of the spotlights and wads of sticky singles peak coyly from the edges of her bikini top and patent leather thong.

Hola mami! Que Linda, she gushes, seductively eying the heave of my breasts as they threaten to spill out of my black lace bustier. She loves how I flirt with masculine and feminine touches in my wardrobe. I usually flaunt my girls for the girls—I like to think it's better for tips—but I'll choose Durangos over Manolos any day. I'm pretty sure that my sheer Mac lip lacquer and the fact that I refuse to leave the house without tracing my eyelids with coal liner qualifies me as a lipstick lesbian, but high femme I am not. I'm more cheerleader than jock, but less sugar than spice.

I can definitely pass for hetero (my ex–boy toys can

attest to that) but always get a rush when a fellow lesbian gives me a subtle smirk on the train, sniffing out my sexuality like a canine cop. The unspoken recognition that our mouths water for the same female delicacies is like sharing a juicy secret.

Tonight, I offset my delicate lingerie top with army-issued fatigue pants, leather motorcycle gloves, and Chuck Taylor All Stars. My mane of untamed, corkscrew curls is swept into a wild, blonde "frohawk." It's obvious that I like to stand out in a crowd.

"Thanks, sexy," I purr. "You killed that last set. Keep moving like that and I might have to spend all my tips on a lap dance before the night is over." We share a wicked giggle as I instinctively start to mix her usual syrupy, crimson-colored concoction.

"Oh please, mami!" she gripes in a thick Cuban accent. "You know I've wanted to be your private dancer for months now."

Now, Red Devil looks undeniably tasty but I'm pretty sure Esquelita's premier go-go girl lusts after more dicks than dykes. One look at those French-tipped talons wrapped around her bottle of Poland Spring confirms what I already knew. Anyone who hopes to dip into me will have to clip the claws and cancel their weekly appointments with the manicurist. I've sexed my share of experimental freaks and although I can't say I regret even one frenzied hump or inexperienced grope of my less than pristine past, these days I want someone who craves pussy as much as I do.

The Vitamin E that I popped earlier suddenly hit me

with a rolling wave. I snatch up a stout bottle of Patron by its stubby neck and chill a shot of silver tequila to balance out my mounting high. I throw back my poison and embark on a mission to the little girls' room. The slimy film that covers the littered floor is a result of hours of bumping and grinding in an unventilated dungeon and makes for a precarious commute to the bathroom.

The cavernous washroom reeks of sex, all the mirrors are completely fogged up, and even the walls are perspiring. A bloated security guard points his flashlight at one of the grimy stalls, "Smells like somebody's getting busy in the champagne room" he announces with a not-so-subtle wink as he passes me a smoking Dutch Master. A quick pull is all the stimulus my inner voyeur needs to take over. Without a word, I slip into the next cubicle for a free peep show.

The pleasure-drenched whimpers turn me on immediately. The sounds are barely audible over Daddy Yankee's booming anthem but the desire is tangible. The lustful lullaby strokes me like a lover's tongue and I close my eyes for a second, savoring the aphrodisiac as it pumps through my veins. Then I cautiously step up onto the toilet seat and peer over the partition, trying to remain unnoticed by my naughty neighbors.

"Oi, oi, oi." My panties dampen.

I recognize Hypnotiq, the source of the intoxicating moans. She's bent over the toilet, one heel stabbing the tiled floor, the other cocked up on the ceramic bowl. Her head is bowed. I yearn for a glimpse of her expression, hidden by the dampened locks that cling to her cheeks.

There she crouches, arms taut, fingers spread against the cold, graffiti-covered wall, dress gathered loosely around her winding hips. Her outstretched digits straddle the words "Ivette y Leticia"—a lonely scrawling that remains a testament to another couples' long-forgotten bliss.

"Ahhh, mami, right there."

Without thinking, I bury my trembling hand in my pants and slip it under my panties. My fingers dip into my wetness and slowly begin to orbit my clit. I can't even blink.

Thug Passion is in full glory standing behind her spread-eagled conquest, her fingers feverishly kneading the fleshy, heart-shaped vessel as it rocks into her. She slides the brim of her Yankee cap to the back and rips aside Hypnotiq's love-soaked thong to accommodate her strap-on. Then she grips her trembling *chichos* (love handles) for leverage and glides herself in deeper.

My breath quickens. My heart thumps. My fingers waltz faster. I begin to match their spastic rhythm.

Their dance is beautiful and organic, not some pseudo simulation of hetero sex. Passion's flexible rubber rod is more than a prosthetic limb; it's an extension of her tiny erection. She moans with such genuine urgency that you'd think her magic stick was covered with a web of nerve endings. If I didn't know from experience that she was actually being aroused by the suction of the rubber base against her clit, I would swear that Tinkerbell had worked some magic and turned it into a real, live dick.

Hypnotiq frantically grabs at the fabric of the Dickie's behind her, hungry for deeper thrusts. Her swollen pussy lips devour the silicone dick, greedily sucking on it like it's a Twizzler. When Passion finds that sensitive, spongy nook, it triggers a roaring climax; she abandons her steady rhythm and begins to buck uncontrollably. I watch gap-jawed as the ecstasy seeps from her pores and drips down her face. Hypnotiq sighs deeply as her partner reluctantly withdraws, leaving the juicy evidence of her orgasm still clinging to the shaft, regretful to say good-bye.

An impatient bang at my stall door interrupts my desperate attempt at self-stimulation and instantly snaps me back to reality. I snatch my hand from between my legs with a jerk and almost slip off the toilet. After avoiding a nasty spill, I try to collect myself and ease the frustration of my sexcapade's abrupt finale. My privates must be bright blue from all the unreleased excitement bubbling down south. I guiltily slink out of the stall and make my way through the crowded bathroom. This feels more like premature evacuation!

Outside, I wade through the sea of dancing bodies, my panties sloshing against my pussy with each step. As much as I want to finish what I started I've got to return to my thirsty customers. Little do they know I'm just as parched as they are—only I'm craving a sip of something that can't be served in a cup.

I'm so distracted that I bump right into my favorite patron, Red Stripe. My hand unintentionally brushes against her chest.

My cheeks get warm.

"My bad," she says, looking down at my lingering

touch with a wicked grin. "Where you been? You're the only one I want giving me a Screaming Orgasm."

My clit jumps.

She continues to nurse her bottle of Jamaican Lager while I start mixing the shot she just requested. I go a little heavy on the vanilla vodka and add just a few dashes of Kahlua, Amaretto, and Irish Cream. Then I shake the creamy potion a little harder than necessary, teasing my admirer with my milk shake.

"You'd better watch mixing those beers with this creamy shit," I warn her like any self-respecting drink slinger would.

"Don't worry," she jokes. "The one thing I know how to do right is lick 'er!"

I spring a leak.

"You're so corny," I say as I walk away, trying to ignore my sopping-wet panties.

A pretty, caramel-dipped honey reaches into her change purse and waves a twenty for my attention.

"What can I get ya, hun?"

"What did you just serve that sexy bitch in the corner?" she demands. "Tell her that her next shot's on me."

"I believe she's got a Buttery Nipple," I answer. *Or two.*

"Um, um, um," she gushes, glaring at Red. "She looks like a butch Alicia Keys."

I couldn't argue with the aggressive vixen. Red is a Columbian cutie that turns her share of heads. Tonight she's wearing a cutoff T-shirt to show off her toned, tattoo-etched shoulders. Intricately woven cornrows snake over her scalp and down her back. Her tough exterior veils a surprisingly tender heart but she's nowhere near a hardcore butch. That's what I like about her. She doesn't get caught up in role-playing or gender bending. She's just being herself—one sexy tomboy.

Her smoldering eyes squint when she smiles and are framed by endless, onyx lashes. Her full, pink mouth is punctuated with a dark beauty mark that sits perfectly between her right nostril and her upper lip. I can't help but imagine her thick soft, lips grazing my...

Red catches me staring. I nearly cream myself. Yup, she's definitely hot.

She accepts the drink and winks her appreciation from where she stands but makes no move to approach her sexy suitor across the bar.

Good girl.

"Last call for alcohol," booms the DJ sending a surge of people to me for one final libation.

Twenty minutes later, the post-party rubble is illuminated by the glaring houselights. Some of the women, not wanting to be remembered with frizzy hair and smudged makeup, scatter like roaches and run for cover in the darkness outside. Others linger, frantic to make at least one love connection. There's a small scuffle near the exit. It's most likely a feud between a couple of studs turning up the machismo to overcompensate for their lack of testosterone. I spot Thug Passion and Hypnotiq, the unknowing participants in my voyeuristic ménage à trois, walking out hand in hand, glowing with post-orgasmic bliss.

My clit screams for attention.

I count my tips and wipe down the bar, absently watching the porno that's playing on the flat screen TV above me. Usually, the oohs and ahhs of male-directed "lesbian" porn just don't do it for me. There's something about a bunch of silicone-stuffed come guzzlers posing as dykes that's just not convincing. Reality is that real girl on girl sex is not always pretty. It can be clumsy, animalistic, and even voracious—but it's usually always sensual.

I can feel her eyes on me as I clean. They turn me on more than the naked women on the screen.

Eventually the club empties. Two hulks stand guard at the front door while my manager counts up the night's profits in the office upstairs. A crew of Mexican busboys runs around, sweeping up the party's aftermath. When the last of the garbage bags have gone out to the dumpster, Red and I are finally left alone.

I can't wait another second. I'm ravenous for her. I need to taste her smile, feel her lips against mine. I'm on her in an instant. Our lips embrace before we do and I swallow her with my kiss. She steals my breath. My eyes flutter shut.

She is delicious.

She pulls away for a moment and time stops. Her hand grabs my chin and steadies my gaze within an inch of hers. My mouth still waters for her tongue but she keeps me firmly where I am, letting my want grow with every shared breath we take until her exhales become my inhales. I try to press my face even closer to hers but she holds strong and caresses the contours of my lips with the tips of her fingers instead.

My heart truly begins to ache and I don't mean that figuratively. I can actually feel a slow burn invading my chest. I hurt with need.

When she finally breaks the spell, our kisses turn chaotic, desperate at times. Her hands are all over me and I still hunger for more of her touch. She grabs a handful of my mane and I can hear the tinkle of the bobby pins as they hit the floor. I grasp her by the back of the neck to draw her closer and the heat between us blisters until her body fuses with mine.

Something flutters beneath my ribcage.

Red lifts me up onto the bar and tickles my collarbone with her tongue. I trace the lines of her tattoo with the tip of my tongue. She shudders. Then she nestles her head into the warmth of my breasts and reaches behind me to remove my top. Her teeth clink against the cold metal of my pierced nipples sending a jolt to my groin.

I draw in a sharp breath through clenched teeth.

My pants can't come off fast enough. Frantically, she undoes my buckle, peels off my cargos, and drops my panties in a wet wad on the bar. My eyes snap open when she pauses and I see that she's frozen before me, basking in my nakedness. I'm powerless under her gaze.

"Please...don't stop," is all I can manage to choke out.

She's immediately drunk with the power that she has over me. Before I realize what is happening, she is reaching over the bar to grab the soda gun from its holster. She aims her weapon at my chest and squeezes the trigger until a trickle of cool water pours out. It washes down the valley of my breasts, swirls around my belly button, and disappears where I wish her mouth were buried. Then she uses the soda to stimulate my clit making my pelvis tilt upward to meet its effervescent rush.

A shiver rakes across my spine.

My seductress can read the impatience that contorts my face and body and takes a moment to savor it before abandoning her water gun and diving into my peach fuzz.

I thrash into her face.

She softly pinches my swollen lips together and slides her tongue between their supple folds. Then she blankets me with it licking up and down—agonizingly slow at first and then lapping faster like a thirsty dog.

I whisper breathy encouragements.

With just the ball of her finger, she plays at the opening of my slit and then slaps at the wetness she collects there. With one hand she cradles my entire pussy and massages its clean-shaven confines. With the other she forms a tripod. She circles my tender knob with her thumb, fucks me with her middle finger and grazes my asshole with her ring finger, all at the same time.

Shit...

Glistening with a rich glaze, my pussy puckers for her and invites her in deeper. She doesn't just pump in and out with rigid fingers; she massages its walls with fluid strokes, exploring. I feel her gesture for me to come closer while her fingers are still buried inside me—she's fondling my G-spot with a familiar intensity, like she's been there before.

Red senses my urgency as the edge of an orgasm tickles my gut. My womb contracts and clamps tightly around her finger, anchoring its heavenly pose.

Fuck!

My cries ricochet through the club as I detonate. I'm left completely limp, quaking in the aftershocks of my orgasm.

My girlfriend scoops me up off the bar and gazes lovingly into my half-closed eyes. I melt into her arms. We've been in love for two years and still act like newlyweds.

"Thanks, baby," I tell her with a peck. She'd played out my bar fantasy perfectly.

"My pleasure," she says with a grin. "Now, come on. It's getting late. We've got to get home and feed our other kitty."

ROOMMATE PRIVILEGES

TRICIA OWENS

TO OUTSIDERS, MY ROOMMATE Erin is one of those girls who seem to have it all. And to a large degree, she is blessed with a lot of things the rest of us lack. She's athletic enough to have won a full volleyball scholarship to our college, UCLA. She's intelligent—despite her rigorous practice schedule she somehow pulls down a 3.8 GPA. She's friendly and beautiful—who wouldn't look twice at a tall, fit brunette with sparkling blue eyes? Erin is amazing; I am constantly agreeing with my friends on that.

What my friends *don't* know, however, and which I, being her roommate, know very well, is that Erin is a drama queen in a roller coaster lesbian relationship that makes *Queer as Folk* look like *Sesame Street*.

To be fair, much of the blame can be placed on her girlfriend. Lauren is the party girl to Erin's collegiate All-American. While Erin is practicing volleyball four hours a day, six days a week, Lauren is promoting socials at the Alpha Phi sorority house. While Erin is studying in the library for finals, Lauren is helping the boys from Sig Ep clean up the toilet paper that's been draped over their house. Erin is at college because she wants to be a pediatrician; Lauren is here to blow her divorced parents' money.

Erin cares too much; Lauren doesn't care enough. Cue music for one corny, overly dramatic lesbian soap opera.

Now me, I don't have a boyfriend at the moment, but I've tried dating a couple of times since starting the fall semester. I avoid drama like the plague—which might explain why the majority of my relationships have sort of fizzled out: I don't fight to keep them. But it's okay, because I'm in a period of life where I enjoy being single. I hang out with my friends, I participate in the campus shooting club, and when Lauren and Erin pressure me, I attend their sorority parties. But for the most part I study and waste my time at the Santa Monica Beach. I have a hell of a tan.

I admit sometimes it isn't as peachy as I'm making it out to be. I'm not gay, but listening to Erin and Lauren make love in the next room (damn those thin walls!) still has its effect on me. Namely, it reminds me that I haven't had sex in a while and it makes me question what could be so good about lesbian sex—because for the life of me, I can't imagine life without a nice hard cock. My vibrator is my best friend and thank God Erin doesn't notice—or chooses not to comment on—how many batteries I go through every month. I love my vibrator, which makes lesbian sex a mystery to me.

So, yes, I guess you can call me bi-curious—this *is* college, after all—but I've limited my lesbian experience to living vicariously through my beautiful roommate and her equally beautiful girlfriend. It's a compromise I am perfectly happy with.

It's Thursday and I've just finished shooting practice. I'm in an easygoing mood—when I enter the apartment I share with Erin only to find Lauren banging pots and pans in our kitchen.

Acquaintances, when they first learn that Erin is a lesbian, often ask me if I've ever developed a crush on her. I can always answer truthfully: no. No, because if I ever did show signs of interest in my roommate, Lauren might beat the living crap out of me.

Okay, that's an exaggeration. Lauren isn't some butch dyke looking for a fight. As I mentioned before, she's beautiful just like Erin, just in a different way. Erin is the kind of girl you'd expect to see on a box of Wheaties. Lauren is the kind of girl you'd see on a billboard for cigarettes. She's got a way of looking at you that's slightly challenging. She looks for your weaknesses not because she plans to exploit them, but because they amuse her. She has very dark green eyes and they can be piercing. She's always struck me as more devious than most people realize.

I'm not thrilled, therefore, to find a pissed-off Lauren in my kitchen. Whatever peace I'd gained through my shooting session evaporates as I drop my backpack beside the counter and listen to her mutter beneath her breath.

"Everything okay?" I ask since it's the obligatory question when someone is throwing a mini-tantrum in your apartment.

"Erin," is all Lauren huffs, but that sums up every fight they've ever had so I nod understandingly.

I grab a SoBe from the fridge, careful not to bump into her as I do so. I don't know why, but for some reason I do my best not to touch Lauren beyond the hugs Erin insists we give each other periodically. Lauren's not unfriendly. I don't think she'd care if I patted her on the arm once in a while. But for some reason I'm hesitant to do it. I'm not like Erin, who's so touchy-feely she borders on being a molester. Touching means something to me.

So I don't touch Lauren.

"Is she in her room?" I ask after taking a sip from the bottle.

Lauren tosses the pan she's holding into the sink with a clatter that makes me wince. She turns around and leans back against the counter, mimicking my position against the fridge.

"She's in there. Being a little princess. Jesus, you'd think someone as gorgeous as her would have more confidence about what she looks like! I mean, come on—how insecure can you be? It's getting old, Taryn."

"I know. I've talked to her about it lots of times," I reply with a sigh. "She's an amazing person. I wished she could see what we see."

Lauren watches me as she says, "She wouldn't let me take dirty pictures of her."

I stare hard into the mouth of my juice bottle. "Oh?"

"She thinks she looks fat, or ugly, or who knows what. I told her no one else is going to see them but she won't do it."

I try to figure out what I should say in response to this and settle with a noncommittal grunt.

"Yeah," Lauren says, as if I'd said the right thing by saying nothing. I glance at her but she's still staring at me with those intense green eyes and I have to go back to inspecting my bottle.

"So you just come back from practice?" Lauren changes the subject as she motions toward my long-sleeved T-shirt. The shooting range is always cold for some reason and I'm one of those people who freeze when the temperature drops below seventy degrees. "How'd you shoot?"

"The same as usual," I reply with a shrug. "Better than everyone else." I grin and Lauren laughs.

"I'll bet you did," she says in a slightly deeper voice. "When you concentrate on something you're like a force of nature."

A compliment from Lauren? A weird tingle shoots through my belly. I hope it's food poisoning.

Lauren stares at me for another minute. "Look, you're

her roommate. You're neutral. Can you go in there and talk to her?"

"Me?" Drama makes my stomach ache like I ate a dozen jalapenos. "You know I don't like getting in the middle of your guys' business, Lauren. She'll calm down and you guys will make up like you always do: loudly."

Lauren smirks. "You can hear us, huh?"

Crap. I'm glad I'm not one of those people who blush easily because my face would be beet-red right now.

"You guys moan and bang on the walls—of course I can hear you," I shoot back. "You guys are worse than . . . well, guys!"

"I guess you wouldn't understand why we're so vocal," Lauren says, "unless you've experienced it for yourself. Sex between women can be intense in a way that's very different from heterosexual sex. Don't knock it 'til you try it, Taryn."

"The way you and Erin go at it, I don't need to experience it for myself. I feel like I'm in there with you two," I quip.

"Reeaally," Lauren murmurs, arching a brow. "And what do you imagine you're doing when you're with us?"

Okay, so I was wrong about not being a blusher. I walk past her out of the kitchen so she can't see how she's rattled me. "I'll check on her," I mumble, "but I'm not promising anything. I'm not a mediator."

"You're the best, Taryn."

"Uh huh, sure."

Lauren follows me to Erin's bedroom. My room-mate doesn't look especially upset. She's lying on her bed dressed in the blue kimono Lauren gave her last Christmas. She's propped up by pillows and using the TV remote to idly flip through channels.

"Hey, Taryn, how was practice?" she asks. Apparently this is a one-sided tantrum or else Erin is pretending nothing's happened between her and her girlfriend.

"Practice was good. I hit 134 out of 150," I tell her. "So what's this I hear about dirty pictures? Why wasn't I invited?" A joke seems like an easy way to diffuse this situation—if there is one.

Erin gives me a dirty look. "Honestly, Taryn, it's not funny."

I sit on the edge of her bed. "Well, it's just pictures for you and Lauren, right? No one else is going to see them so what's the big deal?"

Erin picks at the sash on her kimono. "I know. But I'm not comfortable posing like that. I feel like I'm modeling for *Playboy* or something."

"What if I posed with you?" Lauren suggests from the doorway where she's hovering. Erin's face reflects uncertainty so Lauren plunges on, "Think of how nice that would be, hon. It'd be like soft-core pictures of the two of us. It'd be beautiful."

"That *would* be nice," I add helpfully, "it'd be like a boudoir picture." And I truly do think they would make a lovely, erotic photo. These are two very attractive women. I have not, unfortunately, thought the situation through, otherwise I would have kept my mouth shut.

"It would mean a lot to me," Lauren says softly and I know that will clinch it. Erin likes to fight but she likes making up even more.

"What would we do?" Erin asks, hesitant. She turns off the TV and sets the remote on the nightstand. "Lie here and just . . . pose? Who would take the pictures?"

"Taryn will."

I should have seen it coming. I really should have. I'm an engineering major so I'm pretty good at connecting the dots. Not this time, though. I think my eyebrows get lost in my hairline they shoot up so high.

"*Me*?"

A camera appears over my shoulder. "Sure, you. You're the only one we can trust with this. You're not some perv, after all." Lauren chuckles. "The fact that you're not into girls makes the situation even better. We know you won't be masturbating to this later."

I pull a face. "Not funny, Lauren."

Lauren doesn't care, though. She's whipped off her tank top and dropped her shorts. The only thing she's still wearing is a black string thong. She's in very good shape.

I tear my eyes from the soft pendulous globes of her breasts and her chocolate-colored aureoles and glare at her. "Lauren, I'm not doing this."

But Erin has caught the fever and quickly shrugs off her kimono. Her smaller, perkier breasts say hi to me. I prefer her body to Lauren's—fitter, with nice, curving musculature. Lauren's more voluptuous. I can see her lathered in oil on the cover of *Maxim*. I quickly raise my eyes and find both women smiling at me with various degrees of amusement.

TRICIA OWENS

I make a face. "I'm not shooting porn of you guys."

"Please, Taryn?" Erin whines. "No one else can do this for us and I know you'd do a really good job and make sure the photos aren't disgusting."

"Erin—" I sigh miserably, already knowing she's going to wear me down.

"One roll," she persists. "That's it."

I guess it could be worse. She could have given me a digital camera and then I'd be stuck taking pictures forever.

I groan in defeat. "Fine. One roll. But if you two start getting hot and heavy I'm out of here."

"Don't worry," Lauren says and her voice is lower, deeper. She's twirling a lock of her brown hair around her forefinger. "We'll make sure you're comfortable with everything that happens in this room."

It's not the reassurance I was looking for. It almost sounds like a threat, but I try not to think about it as I stand up and aim the camera at the bed to test the angle.

"Don't do anything gross," I mutter as I adjust my stance. "Innocent heterosexual here. Don't traumatize me."

They laugh and proceed to ignore me. I guess I can't blame them. They're naked and in love. Why bother with me?

They start to kiss and I admit it's not bad. Two women kissing is a lot more sensual than when a man and a woman do it. I take a few close-ups and then take a few full-body shots. Lauren has twined her legs around Erin's, and it's a very nice shot.

And then they start to touch each other. I've known it would happen eventually but the first time Lauren cups Erin's breast and runs her thumb across the nipple I nearly drop the camera. It doesn't get any better when Erin throws back her head and gasps. Goose bumps break out over my skin. I'm glad I'm wearing a long-sleeved shirt so they won't notice. I'm embarrassed by my reaction and hide my face behind the camera.

The touching escalates. As Lauren kisses Erin's throat, her right hand sweeps down Erin's back and curls around her buttock. I accidentally take a photo of Lauren's hand squeezing Erin's ass because I'm so focused on it.

Erin moans and slowly scoots down the bed until her face is level with Lauren's breasts. My mouth goes dry as I watch my roommate lap at Lauren's nipple and coax it into a hard brown berry. Erin sucks it between her lips and I lick my own. Erin nurses at her girlfriend's breast, moaning softly. I raise my eyes and find Lauren watching me. I flush.

"How are the photos turning out?" she asks as she gently guides Erin to suck on her other breast.

I clear my throat before replying, "Good. They're good. Very erotic."

Lauren smirks. Her green eyes are nearly black as she studies me. She reaches down and urges Erin to lift her head. "Hold on, hon. I want to check the angles on these pictures. Don't move."

I'm confused when Lauren uncurls from her lover and stands up. She approaches me, holding out her hand. "Let me have the camera. I want to see something."

I hand it to her gratefully. I'm ready to take a cold shower.

Lauren brings the camera to her eye and aims it at Erin. "Get on the bed with her, Taryn."

I stiffen. "Excuse me?"

"Get on the bed. I want to see how it looks when I'm on there with her." She lowers the camera when I continue to hesitate. "Oh, come, on, Taryn, she's not going to rape you. Just get on the bed and lay there so I can see how it looks."

Of course I don't think Erin's going to attack me. Flustered, I crawl up the bed and lie down stiffly beside my roommate. I can see her naked body from the corner of my eye. Her hand is resting between our bodies on the bedspread.

"Put your faces closer together," Lauren instructs, waving her free hand. "I need to see if the light blocks Erin's face."

"It doesn't," I snap irritably. "I checked for that."

"Just humor me, okay? Sheesh. Someone's homophobic."

The comment annoys me a lot. Homophobic is something I most definitely am *not*.

To prove it I catch Erin behind the head and pull her face to mine. I hold us cheek to cheek, the corners of our mouths barely touching. Her hair smells of Herbal Essences.

"Wait," she murmurs, "my arm's falling asleep."

She shifts and suddenly I feel them: her hard nipples poking against the sleeve of my shirt. Nipples are just nipples. Big deal, I've got 'em, too. But there's sexual energy in the air and it doesn't escape me that Erin's nipples are hard because she has been fooling around with Lauren.

"Have you ever kissed a girl, Taryn?"

I pull my attention away from Erin's nipples and focus on Lauren, who's busy snapping pictures.

"In high school," I say. "For fun. You know. Just to see what it was like."

Lauren lowers the camera. She's smirking, belittling my first lesbian experience. "And what was it like?"

I refuse to bite. "It was like kissing my sister. It didn't do anything for me."

"Too bad it wasn't me," Erin whispers beside me. I turn my head. Her eyes are so close to mine that all I can see are two blue starbursts. She strokes the back of my head. "I would've given you a *good* kiss."

I smile at her. "I'm sure you would have."

"So why not give it to her now, Erin?" Lauren lowers the camera completely. "Just to see. I won't take any pictures or anything. It'll be between us."

"Look, kissing you is no big deal," I say defensively. "I don't need it to be some dirty secret. I'm fine with it. Really." Lauren's homophobia comment still rankles and I want to prove I'm not like that. "Just kiss me, Erin. It's alright."

"Yeah, kiss her," Lauren agrees, but her voice holds a challenge. She doesn't think I'll do it. "Let's see how straight Taryn really is."

Before I can comment on *that*, Erin pulls me forward and just like that we're kissing. It's how I remember it being with a girl—soft and slow, so much so that I can't help wondering when the lips against mine will stiffen and stubble will abrade the edges of my mouth. I wait for the telltale signs of maleness but of course they don't come. Erin continues to kiss me like the girl she is.

And I kind of like it.

But it's not until she pokes her tongue between my lips that I understand that kissing another girl doesn't have to mean kissing your sister.

The slow slither of a wet tongue into my mouth is every bit as erotic as when a guy does it to me. My belly warms and I can feel liquid heat pooling between my legs. When Erin becomes more aggressive and starts to pump her tongue into me I clutch her shoulder reflexively and pull her closer.

I barely notice the bed dip, but I do notice when Lauren brushes my hair away from the back of my neck and begins kissing me there. My entire body jerks as if I've been struck by lightning. I can't help it; the nape of my neck is a major spot for me. I pull my mouth from Erin's and let out a loud gasp.

"Play with us," Erin whispers as she begins kissing my throat. "It won't hurt you. Just this once. We'll make it nice."

I'm aware that Erin and Lauren are one step away from being nymphos. I think that's half the reason why they fight all the time: so they can have make-up sex. I suppose it shouldn't surprise me that they'd try to seduce me, and yet it does. I'm flattered.

I'm also uncertain.

"I don't know what to do," I whisper shyly.

"Mmm, don't worry about that," Lauren chimes in from behind me. Her top hand comes around my chest and cups my breast and squeezes. I buck back into her in surprise and she laughs softly. "I'll tell you everything you need to do, Taryn. You just be a good girl and follow my orders." She nips the side of my neck. "You can be a good girl, can't you?"

I hope she doesn't know how wet that makes me, but I'm pretty sure she does. All I can do is nod.

"I'm going to take off this stupid shirt," she says. "Erin, get her pants."

It's faster than I expected and maybe that's why they're doing it this way. Before I can come up with reasons why we should stop, they've stripped me of my clothes and underwear. I resist the urge to cover myself, though it's difficult. Having a girlfriend see you naked when you're changing is one thing. Having two lesbians in bed with you while you're nude is a whole different story.

"We should have done this a long time ago," Erin says with a smile. "My roommate's a hottie."

I know I'm not but I let her think whatever she wants. I'm too intimidated by this situation to begin an argument. It's all I can do not to pull a sheet over myself.

"How far are you willing to go?" Lauren asks me as she leans over my right side. Erin is on my left. I'd be worried that I was their sole focus but I know this isn't the case. I'm only here to spice up their sex life. It's okay.

I'd rather be an appetizer than the entree when it comes to these two.

"I don't know," I reply honestly. "This is as far as I've gone with another girl."

"I know what I want from you," Erin says suddenly and when I look at her she looks alarmingly determined. "Get on your hands and knees."

When a guy says that, I know what comes next. However, I have no idea with these two. Nervous, I do as instructed, self-conscious of the sway of my breasts and the vulnerability of my backside. Erin's intentions become glaringly obvious when she abruptly flops onto her back on the mattress and slides her feet up so that the soles rest on the bedspread. I'm left looking between her legs at her crotch, which of course I try not to do.

"Look, Erin, I don't know—" I begin, blushing furiously.

"You can't have a proper lesbian experience without muff diving," Lauren declares from behind me. "Do it or I'll throw that vibrator of yours in the trash. It's time your cunt kissed something other than plastic."

I'm mortified. I brace my arms against the mattress. "It's not like that. I have no problems using my fingers—"

"Spread her lips and put your face in there, Taryn. Get dirty, you little priss!"

When I still hesitate, Lauren puts her hand on the back of my head and pushes down hard. And that simple act steals my strength. My arms give up their resistance and drop my face between my roommate's legs.

"Is that what it takes?" Lauren whispers behind me.

"You need me to force you to do this, Taryn? I can do that. I'm *very* good at making girls do what I want, hon."

Oh . . . no. I start breathing faster because she's right. I'd rather take the cop-out and pretend I'm doing this because Lauren is making me do it. Maybe that's what I've always liked. I'm submissive with men but I never thought about what role I would take if I were with a woman. Lauren's hand in my hair, holding my face down to another woman's pussy, is my answer.

My mouth hovers bare centimeters from Erin's skin. She shaves so she's smooth here. Her skin glistens like wet vinyl. The smell of her—it's intoxicating, musky, and sexy in a way I can't describe. It reminds me of myself and for some reason that turns me on.

Lauren's lips are against my ear as she whispers, "Lick my girlfriend's clit, Taryn. Lick it and suck it and roll your tongue around it. Pretend you're chasing a marble." She gently, slowly thrusts her tongue into my ear canal and I gasp, inhaling more of Erin's scent. "Before I let you leave this room, I'm going to teach you to eat pussy like you've been a dyke all your life. I'm gonna make you crave it, Taryn."

Her words alarm and excite me. I can't remember when I've last been this turned on. My face is flushed with heat and I can feel the wetness between my legs. The throbbing down there makes me groan and anxiously roll my hips.

"I'm getting you hot, aren't I?" she continues lustfully. "I can tell by the way you're trembling. You're nothing but a slut, Taryn. That's good because you should see what

Erin looks like. She wants your straight-girl mouth to eat her out. Her fingers are clutching the sheets and her breasts are pink. She wants to feel your tongue, Taryn. Don't make her wait for it. Don't make her beg."

Yet a twisted part of me thinks that's exactly what I want. I want to hear Erin beg me to lick her pussy. I want her to be hot for *me*. She's gorgeous and she's sexy and I don't need to be a lesbian to appreciate what she is.

Lauren bites my earlobe, making me yelp. "Lick her, Taryn. Slide that tongue of yours through my girlfriend's pussy."

I groan, embarrassed by how strong my lust is. I blow experimentally across Erin's damp flesh and she *moans*. Oh, god.

"That's it," Lauren whispers in a voice that's thick with sin. "Keep going, little girl. Lap her up like the nasty kitten you are."

Shaking, I stick out my tongue and run it lightly across her inner folds. I barely touch her, yet Erin squeals and pushes her hips up against my mouth before I can turn away. Lauren holds my head in place as Erin grinds up against me, smearing her juices across my lips and nose. It's so raunchy and unexpected that I let out a moan and Lauren just tightens her grip in my hair.

"You like it dirty, don't you, Taryn? You like having a girl ride your face."

I feel like I'm going to have an orgasm at any second.

"If you make her come I might consider doing the same to you," Lauren tells me. I shudder like a flag in the wind. "I think it'd be hot to be the first girl to stick her tongue between your legs, Taryn." She laughs and her voice is rich and husky. "I know you've never had another girl taste you, another girl force you to come. I'd love to change that. I'd love to be the fantasy you use when you're burning up that vibrator of yours."

Her dirty talk kills me. I didn't know girls could talk like guys but I should have expected it of Lauren. She's always been the dangerous one in my mind, but the danger wasn't physical. It has always been this—of her overwhelming me sexually. I've feared it all along.

Fantasized about it.

I moan when she drapes herself across my back. Her nipples drag like diamonds across my shoulder blades. Is there anything more erotic than that feeling? Possibly. As I lick out her girlfriend, Lauren reaches around me and begins massaging my breasts. Her fingers tweak and roll my nipples and it makes my entire body twist and turn in pleasure. I can feel her breath against the back of my neck. I can feel the trimmed hair of her mound rubbing against my ass. I spread my legs and I beg the best way I can while my mouth is otherwise engaged.

"I'm gonna taste you," Lauren whispers into my ear and it's all I can do not to collapse in a quivering heap.

She slides down my body, deliberately dragging her nipples down my skin in twin trails of fire. I feel Lauren's hands on my ass, squeezing and caressing the globes. Her palms are soft, her fingers thin and elegant, underscoring that this is a *woman* looking at my intimate parts. When she pushes my cheeks apart I'm so excited I burrow my tongue into Erin's hole, making her gasp. Erin may be closer to orgasm at this moment but I have a feeling that once Lauren touches me, I'll win this particular race.

Her thumbs find me first, parting my outer lips. The barest brush of her fingers across my sex makes my head spin and I moan like some kind of whore. Erin loves the vibration and shoves my face harder into her crotch. My face is so deep into her pussy that I'm practically breathing through her.

Then I feel it: a delicate swirl that I at first assume is her finger again. But it returns and it's too soft, too agile . . . too hot. I cry out when her tongue finds my clit and curls around it like a question mark. She sucks me, laps at me. She lashes her tongue back and forth across that hard button as if she's spanking it. I can't think. I can't breathe. All I can do is spread my legs wider and push my hips back and thrust my tongue into Erin as deeply as I can.

Erin's fingers yank my hair. I hear her give a strangled cry—and then her taste is flooding my tongue. I can't pull away; she's got a death grip on my hair. I keep my face buried where she wants it and slurp up her juices while Lauren returns the favor and fucks me senseless with her tongue.

My legs tremble. My feet begin to tingle. I know I'm almost there. Lauren moves her lips away for a second and slides her middle finger all the way inside me . . . and I break.

I cry out against Erin and buck like a rodeo horse. Lauren holds on to me and flicks me with her tongue to draw it out—out—until it's too much and I twist myself away from her mouth. She releases me at the same time

Erin uncurls her fingers from my hair. I fall to my side on the bed and gasp for breath. I feel like a big wet mess and yet it's incredible.

"Take care of me," I hear Lauren moan. Erin crawls over me to her girlfriend and by the smacking sounds that follow I know Erin is taking *very* good care of Lauren. I lay with my eyes closed and listen. It's just like lying in my own room, eavesdropping with a glass held to the wall. I won't tell them that I do that, though.

They might think I'm a lesbian.

DRAGON'S FLY
AUNT FANNY

TONIGHT'S MY NIGHT, MAX thought as she carefully clipped her hair in front of the bathroom mirror. I either come home with the crown, or I give it up forever. I swear.

Tossing the clippings into a bowl, Max continued chopping the hair into small shreds. Then she showered and wrapped a wide Ace bandage around her already small breasts, tightening it until she was as flat as possible, but could still breathe. She pulled on her tightest pair of packing briefs, and tucked Dudley into place between her thighs. Made of softly pliable silicone, Dudley filled out a pair of jeans nicely, and almost always came in handy.

Max's full hips were always a problem. Thank God for pleated slacks. And long jackets with padded shoulders. And suspenders instead of belts. They gave Max an old-world Chicago gangster look, which she was completing tonight with a sharp black fedora and spats.

All those dance lessons she'd taken twenty years ago, when her mother insisted, had finally paid off. Who knew that little Maxine Smith, who wore pink tutus and toe slippers, would one day strut her stuff in drag? She laughed out loud as she used a tube of brown lipstick to paint on sideburns and a mustache. Max spread spirit gum over the same area and began carefully applying bits of shredded hair. Then she went to work on her stage makeup.

Not every king went this far, but Max had a strong drive to look her finest. She applied a light base, then penciled in her eyebrows, thickening them. She applied a thin line of black eyeliner, and darkened her lashes, making her clear gray eyes appear bigger, darker, more soulful. She scrutinized her reflection, grinning. Damn she looked fine.

Max glared at the clock, which told her she should have left ten minutes ago. She hurried out the door, jumped into her renovated '68 Mustang convertible, glad she'd put the top up when she got home from work. The wind in her face just didn't help facial hair hold up.

It amused her, and sometimes worried her, that

someone from Baxter, Burnham, and Smith would one day see and recognize her. But her fellow accountants would never believe it possible that the tightly knit little woman they worked with every day could transform into a man, and that alone would disguise her from anyone she might know. Besides, she figured, if they were somewhere she was performing, then they'd come to see a drag show and were probably gay themselves. Blackmail works both ways.

Georgie's was already jumping, and the huge muscular bartender trumpeted at Max as she sprinted through the door, "Shake it up, Dragon. Show starts in ten minutes and you're the leadoff. Check in downstairs with Michael immediately." A third of the patrons were straight, but just the sight of Georgie behind the bar was enough to keep everyone gay friendly. Rumor had it the big man had broken a few ribs and at least two noses in his time.

"Send me down a Heineken," tossed Max over her shoulder as she hustled through the crowd. "Hell, make it two." She maneuvered her way through the people around the bar, threading her way through the tables to the door leading downstairs. A hand lettered sign read: Performers Only. She shoved it open and started down the cement stairs.

It was at this moment that Dragon always made his grand appearance. Each footfall farther down into the basement of dressing rooms, props, and costumes brought Dragon up from deep within Max. He surged into her skin until she disappeared in the dark recesses of his mind.

Dragon was fierce, sexy, demanding, and powerful. He was the best drag-king dancer in the city and he knew it. His tips always doubled, if not tripled, the other dancers in a show. Dragon's following was loyal and passionate. Devotees often decorated his bed in the morning, but by then Max was back and the pretty young women with hangovers disappeared like farts in a tornado, completely uninterested in the plain faced, buttoned up accountant. Max sometimes hated Dragon. And Dragon was openly disdainful of Max. Each wondered on occasion if they should seek professional help.

"Dragon, baby, you're late," prissed Michael, fussing over the wig of Chi Chi LaFemme, tonight's MC. He paused long enough to run his eye appreciatively over Dragon's ensemble. "Get your music to the DJ on the johnny double," he ordered with a wink. "You're going to kick off tonight's competition."

"I heard," playfully grumbled Dragon, just as one of the bar fairies appeared with a tray laden with various beers. He snatched up two Heinekens and threw a five on the tray. Leaning back his head, Dragon guzzled his first beer without pausing, then tossed the bottle in the recycling can.

He went back up the stairs to the DJ's booth, delivering his CD for the evening into Monica's hands personally. Dragon never took chances with his music.

"Good luck, Dragon." Monica leered at the drag king, then leaned over, and bussed him on the cheek. She laughed and spit out a loose hair or two that got in her mouth. "You look great."

"Thanks, Mon," Dragon answered casually, leaning in and taking another, more leisurely kiss. "It's my night to win." He released her and left the booth.

It *is* my night to win, Dragon thought fiercely. He'd been runner-up the first year and, still piqued, declined to compete the second. During the third year he'd faced fierce competition from some upstart calling himself Leonardo, and lost during the style event. The fourth year he'd excelled in style, but lost during the dance portion. This year Dragon had it all, and he'd rehearsed each performance until he felt Broadway worthy. Snap.

He could do this. Because if he didn't, Dragon was hanging up his dancing shoes, never to perform again.

"Hey bud," he heard Marcos' gruff voice. Turning, he saw the dapper dancer, also dressed and ready for the competition. Marcos had won four years earlier, and was wicked good competition. He was wearing a black tuxedo, complete with scarlet bow tie, cummerbund, and pocket hankie. His hair was a straight up crop, dark brown with blond tips. A pair of impenetrable blue aviator glasses gave Marcos the air of an international spy.

"Hey," Dragon tossed back. "You're lookin' good tonight, Marcos."

"Thanks, man," said Marcos, giving Dragon a thorough up and down inspection. "You're looking pretty sharp your own self." He reached out and plucked one of Dragon's suspenders, letting it slap back in place. "Nice touch."

Dragon liked Marcos. But he really wanted to win tonight too. Finally he forced himself to say, "Break a leg, Marcos," which was as good as wishing him the drag king title.

"Same to you, bro," said Marcos throwing a fake punch to his arm, which wasn't the same thing at all. But Dragon had the edge of going first—first chance to impress. He had to set the bar so high that every performance after his paled by comparison.

Glad-handing with the crowd, Dragon greeted people, left and right, as he headed backstage. Chugging half his second beer, he felt liquid fire ignite his belly. He grabbed the hand of a woman he knew from earlier performances and danced a quick step with her to the music blaring from the overhead speakers. He drank in her surprised eyes as she felt Dudley pressing her inner thigh. Dragon grinned seductively, making his dance companion's friends jealous. He released her to them and walked quickly backstage. He was ready. God was he ready.

Chi Chi LeFemme took the stage and Monica immediately stopped the music. People quickly shuffled to their chairs at the bar and tables. Georgie's boasted classy performances, and the audience reflected that. Mostly upscale, well dressed, and nicely perfumed, the crowd listened respectfully as Chi Chi greeted them.

"Good evening, Ladies and Gents," she said with her stunning white smile. Chi Chi was already thirty, but still looked like a teen. In real life she was Jose Moreno, quietly capable auto mechanic at Sears, but by night Miss Chi Chi emerged, a beautiful, fragile butterfly. Tonight she was all in sequins, her long legs encased in black net stockings, her feet in glamorous pumps.

"As you know, tonight marks the fifth annual Drag Queen and King Competition at Georgie's," Chi Chi announced. "Our theme this year is Broadway, and each selection must be from a successful show, past or present. This year's judging panel includes—" Dragon let the beat of his own heart drown out the MC's voice as he prepared for his performance. He shook his arms and legs out, flexing his neck and shoulders.

At last he heard the warm-up strains of his song and Chi Chi announced, "To kick off the dance competition tonight we have Dragon performing "Luck Be a Lady," from *Guys and Dolls*." Dragon tensed his muscles and leapt on stage.

In high school Maxi had performed the role of Sister Sarah Brown in *Guys and Dolls*. She'd hated the role, but her mother had insisted, so she'd auditioned and gotten the part. She'd have much rather been Sky Masterson, and had in fact learned his dance routines and practiced them on her own. That's the experience Dragon drew upon, dancing athletically across the stage, grace in every step.

He danced like one possessed, giving it his all. "Stick with me baby, I'm the fella you came in with," Dragon lip-synched. He moved along the front of the stage, using his male persona and soulful eyes to woo the audience and judges. "Luck, be a lady, tonight!" He threw himself to his knees, casting imaginary dice.

The audience responded wildly. He held the pose a moment longer, then stood to take his bows. Chi Chi had already stepped out on stage, but stepped back again as the applause continued, giving Dragon his due. It had been a fantastic start to the contest.

Per the competition's rules, Dragon ignored the dozens of bills littering the dance floor. This was no regular show, and tips were not allowed. Chi Chi quickly swept them up as Dragon left the stage, once again explaining the policy to the audience and handing the money back. The second drag king, Marcos, took the stage, performing "Some Enchanted Evening" from *South Pacific.* The music followed Dragon as he reached the dressing room he shared with the other kings, each in various states of preparation.

He stood there sizing up his competition. Dragon nodded in turn at the four others he recognized from local competitions, and took special note of the fifth. The thirty something cowboy was slender and tall, with brilliant brown eyes and a close cropped cap of dark curls. He was finishing a full beard in front of the mirror, and their eyes locked in the reflection. He grinned at Dragon, dancing eyes crinkling up at the corners. He turned half way around and threw long arms over the chair.

"I'm Fly. Fly Boi," he said, grinning boldly. His eyes roamed over Dragon, absorbing everything. Fly winked appreciatively.

Dragon recognized his first ever attraction to another king. Usually he only got hot for femmes, plenty of whom vied for his attention. He'd never considered his fellow kings as possible bedfellows. But Fly here, was clearly another story. The cowboy was gorgeous. Warm brown hair and eyes gave his rich olive complexion a European look. His openly flirtatious grin showed even white teeth, and full lips hinted at simmering sensuality.

Dragon narrowed his eyes and gave Fly "the look." He knew from hours in front of the mirror that his clear gray eyes were radiating pure sexual desire. Both drag kings grinned at the same time.

"I need some help taping," Fly said, unfolding from the chair to unbutton his flannel shirt. He pulled it free from a pair of well-worn men's jeans. "I'm on next." Two perfectly shaped breasts leapt into view, swinging freely, nipples erect. Dragon stepped forward immediately.

"Allow me," he purred, grabbing the roll of medical tape and scissors available for the kings. He quickly applied one strip after another until Dallas was flat as a board. He ran his hands over the tape, supposedly smoothing it in place. He felt the restrained breasts beneath his palms, and felt his own pressed tits respond. Dragon's hands lingered until the cowboy pulled away.

Fly quickly buttoned his flannel shirt with a grin of promise. He grabbed a white cowboy hat from a bag at his boot-shod feet, then rapidly climbed the stairs, pausing once to throw back a wink.

"Break a leg," Dragon growled. He watched the handsome king disappear, then turned to preparing for the style portion of the competition. Keep your mind on business, he reminded himself sharply. The opening strains of "Oh What A Beautiful Morning" sounded from above. Curly from *Oklahoma*. Ambitious and clever.

As Dragon finished fixing his makeup, he heard excited applause. Moments later he caught a quick glimpse of Fly as the long, rangy king swung easily back into the dressing room.

"I hear," Dragon called out with a nod of his head upstairs, "you're a crowd favorite." He took a long pull from his Heineken.

Fly, high on success, grinned widely. His face was beautifully handsome. Excited eyes flashed and he did a quick spin, arms extended. "That's me, baby," he crowed as he removed his flannel shirt. "It's a hot job, but somebody's got to do it, eh Dragon?" Fly threw him a seductive wink, stripped to the waist.

Dragon had never wanted anyone more. He did some quick calculations. "The flush of success," he agreed laughing, pulling open his own shirt and letting it dangle from his waistband. He knew his suspenders deftly outlined the subtle swelling of his bandaged breasts.

They weren't alone. Several of the kings in the basement were in various states of undress. There was no fan down in the dressing room. It was an oven.

"I know a place where we can cool down," murmured Dragon discreetly so the others wouldn't hear. "Come with me, Fly. There's at least forty five minutes before I go on, and you've got another ten after that."

Grabbing the Heineken from Dragon's hand, Fly took a long drink, then plopped the empty on the counter. "Lead on, my good man," he said.

Dragon led the way up the back stairs and out into the small fenced patio reserved for performers, open to the night air. A bazillion stars twinkled overhead, but only six were visible through the haze of city lights.

Dragon didn't allow any moments of awkwardness. He turned and swept the good looking cowboy into his arms. He felt strong arms wrapping around him in return and moved in for a kiss. Dragon's mustache brushed Fly's as their lips made contact. Beard bristles tickled something deep in his belly. Dragon kissed hard, using his hands to explore Fly's naked back and waist.

Impulsively, Fly grabbed one of the metal yard chairs and shoved it under the doorknob, bracing its feet against the cement. He turned back into Dragon's arms and slithered down his body until he was crouched crotch high. He looked up, his handsome face grinning widely.

"Let's see if it's as good as promised," he said, patting Dudley through Dragon's slacks. Long fingers slowly undid the zipper of the pleated pin-stripe slacks, *"zzzzip."* The sound reverberated in Dragon's ear, drowning out the sounds of the street traffic on thc other side of the fence. Ecstacy. Who needs drugs?

Fly's fingers tugged the opening wide then reached in and found Dudley, pulling him free. His flesh colored head bounced into the light thrown by the street lamp overhead. Dragon's head spun. He could almost feel the cool night air on his exposed cock.

Looking up sexily, Fly used both hands to pet, stroke, and caress Dudley, being sure to push his curved base into Dragon's clit. Hips thrust forward, and Fly accommodatingly swallowed the cock, grinning wickedly around it. A pointed pink tongue licked the silicone flesh. Dragon groaned, willing himself to feel it.

Soon he needed more, so he pulled Fly up on his feet,

eagerly undoing the button fly jeans, shoving them down around the cowboy's lean thighs. Fly was strapped; a realistic dildo nestled between his thighs.

Dragon pulled him into a sensual hug, their taped breasts and dangling dildos dueling in the dark. Fly's well rounded ass fit neatly into his hands as Dragon kissed him hard, tongue thrusting roughly between parted lips.

Walking them both backward, Dragon stopped in front of a long wooden bench. He turned Fly around and leaned him forward, gasping with appreciation as the drag king's ass rose and swelled before his eyes, outlined by thin leather straps. Fly grasped the bench with both hands, then spread his feet as wide as his bunched jeans would allow. Dragon could see the dildo hanging between his legs.

Stroking Fly's bottom, Dragon ran first one and then the other hand over his exposed pussy. Teasing strokes increased in intensity until Fly's hot desire spilled out of flushed nether lips.

Looking over his shoulder up at Dragon hovering over him, Fly moaned, "Fuck me, baby!"

Dragon plunged into Fly's wet cunt, sighing in satisfaction as he took it up to the hilt. Placing one hand on either butt cheek, he rode the cowboy's sweet pussy, enjoying the wet sounds of their fucking in the night. Fly moaned beneath him, stroking his cock with one hand, with the other bracing himself on the bench.

Passion surged within him, and Dragon began fucking Fly harder than he'd ever fucked anyone before. He thrust his cock in and out of him faster and deeper. "Yes, baby," growled Fly, rearing his ass back to take everything he had to give.

Dragon pounded his hips forward and back, allowing Dudley's base to stimulate himself as well as his lover. His clit throbbed, his crushed breasts ached, and somehow his cock became an extension of them all. He leaned forward and grabbed Fly's shoulders, holding them as he slammed his cock home, over and over again until Fly cried out into the night, cresting madly. Dragon rocked on until he found his own release, pulling the cowboy's ass back into his hips and grinding fiercely. He raised his head and howled at the night sky, sheer animal pleasure pouring from him.

"Damned queers," they heard a disembodied voice from over the fence. The two drag kings started, pulling apart and looking around guiltily. Then they laughed in each others' arms.

"Well," announced Fly, yanking his jeans back up and tucking his cock and shirt back in, "I feel great. How about you?"

Dragon thought about that as he tucked Dudley back in. He zipped up, then stood still watching Fly. "I feel," he said, then stopped. "I feel fantastic," he announced, surprised to find it true. Too often sex left him feeling empty, drained. Instead he felt energized, eager to see what came next. He grinned at Fly, then glanced at his watch. "We better get back downstairs and see where we are in the lineup," he said.

On the way back to the dressing room, Dragon grinned watching Fly walk in front of him. Suddenly the competition wasn't nearly as important as it had once seemed. If anything, he was half hoping that if he didn't win, that Fly would. His pleasure in the potential success of his lover made him proud, and he found himself wanting someone else to be happy, even if it was at his own expense.

And he wasn't the only one thinking that. Deep inside his mind he heard Max echoing the sentiment. For the first time in forever, Dragon and Max agreed.

The rest of the competition went by in a blur. Dragon performed, then stood in the wings so he could watch Fly when it was his turn. He led the applause, thrilled at the reception his lover was receiving from the audience. They hugged in the wings, and swung downstairs to wait for the finale together.

They chatted for over an hour, finding many things in common. They made three dates. On the first they'd go fishing. On the second they'd try a new Mexican food restaurant, and on the third they planned to water ski. The time flew by. Dragon was surprised to find he'd only nursed a single beer during their conversation. Usually after a show he had six or seven.

Michael rounded everyone up for the grand crowning of the king and queen. The six kings and eight queens lined up on the stage, alternating genders, blinking in the stage lights. Everyone was excited, hopeful, and afraid of public humiliation. They gripped each others' hands and awaited the judges' pleasure. Some jittered, some stood calmly. Some laughed, and some seemed ready to cry.

Miss Chi Chi LaFemme approached the mic with two

envelopes in her hand. She made a few silly jokes, then took pity on the waiting competitors, and announced the runners-up. Neither Dragon nor Fly was named. They looked at each other from their places along the line. Fly grinned and nodded at Dragon.

Wondering how he'd feel if he lost, Dragon nodded back at Fly. Proud, he hoped. He grinned at his lover, his eyes twinkling brightly.

"And this year's new Georgie's Drag Queen and King are—" said Miss Chi Chi, fumbling with the envelope. "Oh, I'm so sexcited," she simpered, earning a laugh. She quickly read the card enclosed, then reread it. "May I present our new Queen," she said, grinning widely and gesturing behind her at the row of hopefuls, "Amanda B. Reckonedwyth!" The tall statuesque queen stepped forward, raising her gloved hand to wave at the audience, who thundered their applause. Miss Chi Chi handed her a purple satin sash, and crowned her with a glittering tiara. Amanda was quickly surrounded by congratulating queens who soon swept themselves off to one side of the stage, leaving the kings standing alone.

They glanced nervously at each other, then struck individual poses of composure. As one, they stared at Miss Chi Chi, who grinned saucily back at them.

"Amanda will be joined at court by Georgie's Drag King," drawled the MC. "Or in this case, Drag Kings. Dragon and Fly Boi have tied, and will share the title!" She gestured to the kings, who stepped forward beaming. Fly was handed the crown, which he promptly put on. Dragon was soon wearing the sash. They hugged each other and were swarmed by not only the other kings, but the queens as well. The audience howled their approval.

Later that night they made love again, finally unwrapping and unstrapping. They enjoyed each others' womanliness, exploring the curves, hills, and valleys of each other thoroughly. Each orgasmed twice before they rested. After a short nap they rose together to wash.

"Of course, there's a side of me you haven't seen yet," Fly announced, using the washcloth and solvent Dragon gave him to clean up. "I don't wear this stuff all the time."

"Me neither," said Dragon, Max rising as the makeup washed away. "I'm actually a mild mannered accountant. I wear dresses and heels to work." She turned, waiting to judge Fly's reaction to her scrubbed, plain, female face.

"I know," said Fly looking up slowly with her own clean, surprisingly familiar face. "I work two offices down from you." She stuck out her hand. "Anita Baxter, of Baxter, Burnham, and Smith. It's me, Maxine. Your partner."

WIDE AWAKE
LIEZL SARTO

WIDE AWAKE. I DON'T remember what woke me but I do recall what I saw. Serene, she was next to me, sleeping. Our days had been so taxing on the both of us that we almost collapsed on the bed the minute we got home. Slipping out of our clothes and into our pajamas, we climbed into bed. The slight butch in me loves to sleep in boxers and a wife-beater while she prefers her little bikini cut panties and spaghetti-string tank top. She was sleeping on my arm and her back was facing toward me. My eyes drifted over her body as if they were gently caressing her skin. Her soft and short brown hair always tickles my nose when we sleep. My eyes kept gliding over her from the side of her sexy neck, to her chiseled back, hourglass shape, down to her smooth stems that are always held up by the most expensive stilettos imaginable. I saw her. I needed her. I wanted her. *But she's sleeping so peacefully*, I thought to myself as I wrapped my arm back around her waist. She let out a little moan and placed her hand over mine, acknowledging that I was there. I glanced at the clock: 2:35 A.M. *Shit, I can't sleep.*

Wide awake. Minutes seemed to pass by like hours. Holding her, the comfort of her being in my arms felt like excruciating pain, torment because the need was growing rapidly within me. The warmth she gave off was heating me to my inner core. Suddenly, she moved her head slightly and her hair slowly descended onto the pillow as if it were slow motion, exposing her bare neck to me. Fate was teasing me. I slowly progressed to kiss the back of her neck, planning my next move.

Wide awake. I started raking my fingers across her stomach slowly, hoping the movement would slowly wake her. She uttered, *Mmmm...*, as I continued to caress her neck with my lips. My fingers played with her navel gently as she started to rub my arm with her hand. My hand wandered over her torso as my lips kissed her behind her ear and down the backside of her neck. I felt myself getting wet. I want her.

Heat seemed to reside in my head, leaving me dizzy and hot all over my body. Her tight firm ass was pressed against my crotch. My hand slipped into her tank top, slowly moving up her torso. I felt her heavy breathing as her chest heaved deeper and deeper, hot air escaping through her lips in muted gasps. Soft, silky, velvety smooth skin ran underneath my hand. She was voluptuous and built like no other woman. Her breasts were hills of heaven within my reach. Searching to reach the peak, I found it. Pink, hard and in my fingertips. She turned to face me. Her green eyes sparkled in the moonlight and the slight smirk on her face told me she wanted more. I was so wet. Her lips found mine, exchanges of breaths, dancing of tongues. Meanwhile, I rolled her nipple with my fingers, pinching, rubbing her breasts to make her quiver.

My hand changed direction. Down. Down, all I could think of was down. The kissing got deeper. Breathing got heavier. Her legs slowly parted as I approached my destination. My hand was on her hip, outer thigh, inner thigh, slowly grazing it with my fingertips. I could feel the heat from her cunt. I rubbed her hard over her panties. She was wet. The feel of her hot wet mouth melting into mine was amazing. The way her tongue moved about my mouth, the pressure that was exerted when she sucked and bit on my lower lip made me weak. Her moans drove me crazy, sending shocks down to my aching pussy. My hand slipped into her panties, into the hot slippery paradise. My finger felt its way into her pussy lips, the heat, and the smell, onto her engorged clit. I felt throbbing in my pussy, wanting to be touched as well, but I wanted to please her first. I wanted her to be satisfied.

Her lips were so sweet. Slowly her tongue danced with mine. Her hips were slowly moving with my fingers. They glided so easily up and down with gentle pressure. She lay on top of me, with her back against my stomach; legs spread wide apart, our legs entangled with each other's. She wrapped her arm back around my neck while we kissed, pulling me in more, her moaning, short breaths telling me that she wanted more. Her hips moved in a rhythmic pattern with my hand. I could feel her legs tensing up as I moved inside her. Short gasps escaped her mouth. Her pussy got soaking wet; I could feel it through my boxers. Her warm, wet, smooth-shaved mound felt incredible.

She pulled out my hand from her hot, sticky cunt and brought it to her lips, licking them clean. She flipped me over and straddled me hard, kissing me deeply; her tongue was at the back of my throat. My arms held her tight, and having her so hard against me made me the horniest I'd ever been. She sat up and removed her tank top, exposing her perfect breasts to me. I placed my hands on them, kneading them while she grinded against me. She looked me dead in the eye and said with her low sexy tone, "I'm not going to stop riding you 'til you can't take it anymore." God, she looked amazing when she rode me, her perfect body and perfect bed hair.

Just the thought of our hot pussies rubbing against each other almost made me come. The throbbing got worse and worse as we continued to kiss, grind, and feel each other all over. She slowly slipped her hands into the slit of my boxers, teasing me here and there with her fingertips. She moaned, "Mmm…baby, you're so wet, I want to taste you so bad—" She stopped abruptly and sat up, glamorous in the moonlight. She pulled off my tank top to expose my breasts and leaned forward to suck on them. Her hot mouth over my nipple sent shocks through me. Meanwhile she undid her straddle so her stomach was between my legs. Moving her body off to the side she slowly maneuvered her hand into my boxers.

"Baby, you are so wet!" she whispered as she sucked on my tit. "Let me see if I can do something about it—" My mind was exasperated by this point, not knowing where to concentrate my desires. My hand ran over her bare back and through her hair as her fingers ran through my labia, exciting my clit more and more, entering me little by little. Her mouth slowly descended down my body, kissing my navel and tonguing it to prolong her overdue arrival to her destination.

"Baby, please... I need you," I begged. Her hands worked my boxers off me and guided my thighs wide apart. Feeling her breathe so close to me was driving me wild. Her fingers pulled my labia apart and I felt the tip of her hot tongue on me, sending sensations all over my body. The hot air exhaled onto my clit sent shivers down my spine. Slowly her fingers entered one by one, moving all around. Her tongue moved wilder in me, harder and harder. I felt like I was paralyzed: toes curled, ass tight, hands grabbing at the sheets until I felt it coming. Her tongue moved up and down with absolute accuracy; she knows what I like. The pressure she put on was harder and harder while her fingers worked me faster and faster. The release I'd been waiting for! "Yes, oh my God baby! Shit! Fuck!" It was so fucking good, I couldn't stop shaking! I felt like I came forever! Convulsion after convulsion, I finally came down from my high.

She climbed up on top of me, kissing me with my own taste all over her mouth. She straddled me once again and said, "My turn." I worked her panties off her slowly, making her wait as we kissed harder and harder. She made her way north, and I knew what she wanted. "Come on, baby, I've been wanting to taste you all night! You keep teasing me!"

"Ask and you shall receive," she said and then straddled my head as she held onto the headboard. The moment my tongue entered her pussy lips, she let out a big gasp as if her anticipation had been finally fulfilled. She tasted so sweet. My hands were all over her nice ass, guiding her hips to the rhythm of my tongue. She started to moan louder and louder and she started to ride my face harder and harder. I was sucking at her labia, flicking my tongue gently at her clit while my fingers entered her. She rode faster and faster as her breathing got very deep and fast. I knew she was almost there when she tightened her ass.

"Mmmm, baby!!!" She whispered loudly as moans escaped from her mouth. I could feel her body shaking with pleasure from her orgasms.

She climbed off me and lay next to me exhausted. Having known her for so long, I knew we were far from being done.

"I'll be right back, baby," I said on my way to the bathroom to put on the strappy. When I came back, I saw her fingering herself.

"Cheater!" I shouted and pointed at her as she laughed

with the cutest smile in the world. I climbed on top of her, kissing her passionately.

I was between her legs but not inside her; it was my turn to tease. I love her. I love every bit of her. I love her well-sculpted jawline; I ran my lips over it. Moving up to nibble at her earlobes, I kissed behind her ear while grinding against her as if I were in her.

"Mmm... baby," she moaned. My lips and tongue left a trail, following down her slender, sexy neck to the hollows at the bottom. Kissing her chest as my hand grabbed onto one of her huge tits, grinding myself against her, I took in her hard nipple. So sweet, I sucked on it hard and bit down gently as my free hand teased her clit.

"Mmm.... Baby, I'm so fucking wet... I'm aching for you!" she crooned as her hands wandered down my bare back, making me crazy. Slowly I placed the head in, barely entering, putting pressure to make her want it more and more. A few inches in to make her gasp out of control. She couldn't stand the wait any longer and wrapped her legs around me, making me thrust into her.

"Oh fuck...mmm," she moaned as she bit her lower lip. Thrust after thrust her moans got louder and louder.

"Baby, I'm almost there! Faster!" I slowed down, keeping her on the edge of climaxing. Every gentle move was magnified. We kissed harder. Her arms wrapped around my neck. Slowly they made their way down my back to grab my ass.

"Shit... oh my God! Baby, you feel so good!" I went in and out of her slowly, keeping her on the edge of coming. Her legs loosened around me a bit as her hands ran through my hair and held me close. Suddenly she shouted, "FUCK! Faster, baby!" as she wrapped her arms around me hard. I felt her hips buck and I thrust as fast and hard as I can. Her moans got high pitched as she came. I was getting tired from all the movement but she was still coming. She started to scream, "OH GOD! OH GOD! Mmm, BABY! FUCK!"

Exhausted, I climbed off her and lay next to her. I lay on my back staring at the ceiling, tired. She lay on her side, her head propped up by her hand with her elbow bent in an acute angle. She was looking at me, tracing the outline of my breasts with her fingertips.

"God, baby, that was amazing!" She whispered to me as she leaned in to kiss me. We kissed tenderly but passionately, deep and slow. She slowly climbed on top of me, one of her favorite positions and started to ride me.

"God, baby, you're so beautiful!" I told her as she was riding me, her hair leaning away from her face toward me. Her breath quickened with short gasps released. She rode me harder and harder and the pressure was building up against me so well that I start to feel it also. I felt her pace accelerate when her hips started bucking again. Just hearing her moan and come drove me crazy.

"God, baby—" was uttered from her lips as her body convulsed intensely. She lay on top of me, exhausted. "Damn, baby, you drive me crazy!!!" She said to me in short pants as she tried to catch her breath.

I kissed her and rolled her over so she was lying on her stomach facedown. "Mmmm..." was muttered from her lips. I straddled her and started to massage her shoulders and neck, planting kisses in all the sweet spots I'd found over the years. Kissing the back of her neck, up behind her ear and back down again. I knew she loved it; it's one of her favorite spots and positions. I slowly maneuvered myself so I could get between her legs, inserting the head in from behind. Only inches in, I made sure I could stimulate her G-spot. Her moans told me I was doing a good job. She plead "deeper, baby." I slowly entered her inch by inch, letting her aching pussy grab and pull me in more. I moved in and out of her slowly. I felt hot and sweaty all over. The rubbing of our hot bodies was driving me insane, leaving me with a familiar dizziness. A loud moan shot out of her mouth. I could feel her legs starting to tense up as I moved faster and faster. She uttered "UHHHH.........baby—" as I moved rapidly in and out of her while she came for the last time of the night. I kissed her neck, the side of her cheek, and I withdrew. We both rolled over to our sides kissing and holding each other, knowing that we both needed each other.

She kissed me on the cheek, helping me undo the strap-on and threw it to the floor. I rolled onto my back exhausted as she positioned herself next to me, placing her head next to mine as her arm wrapped about my middle. I kissed her forehead and wrapped my arm around her. Her warmth eased me into serenity. My eyelids got heavier and heavier. I could feel my heartbeat slowing down, but pulsing in my head. I was off into a daze, hearing her whisper to me, "I love you, baby." I was no longer awake.

SMOKE BREAK
RACHEL KRAMER BUSSEL

I'M SITTING NEXT TO a stranger in Tompkins Square Park when she takes the long, skinny stick and props it between her lips. She does it with a practiced ease, a lifelong addiction that suddenly, no matter how many Surgeon General's warnings I've read, I want to be a part of too. I inch slightly closer as she strikes the match against the thin cardboard strip and a flame explodes. I have a book propped in front of me but hold my finger between its pages and look over at her as she touches the glowing orange to the end of the smoke and inhales. I can practically feel her satisfaction, though she's too

61

cool to smile. I turn my head slightly so as not to look so obvious. I'm intrigued, fascinated, and covetous, of both the smoke and the girl. She's wearing ragged jeans with strategically torn holes, giant black platform shoes, and a black hoodie. I can't really see her body, but it's her face that makes me want to get to know her better. Her eyes are lined with dark, angry black, her lips a bold red, the black hair shiny but mussed, an imperfect Bettie Page. She's smoking like she's mad at her cigarette—or the world, yet I also sense a calming peace to her. I don't know what it is about her, but I can't look away.

I quit smoking five years ago and have rarely been tempted, but this girl defines tempting. She has that air of East Village cool, like she doesn't care what anyone thinks of her, but I can see her sneaking peeks at me out of the corner of my eye, and I'm glad I've worn my favorite purple fishnets, snazzy black sneakers, and little black dress, even just for a walk in the park. I try to read my mystery, but keep getting distracted by the little puffs of breath I hear coming from her mouth. I always tell myself it'll be good day if I just pick the right panties (baby blue boyshorts today) and the right tights, one of my little quirks that make me feel better when everything else has gone to hell in a handbasket and I want to pack up and move—to Chicago or Boston or Omaha, for that matter, anywhere but my own crowded, crazy, incestuous city. Yet I stay, because for every moment I spend bemoaning the smallness of the dyke community and my inability to find someone who hasn't slept with my ex's ex or some variation thereof, I meet a girl like this one, who simply makes me forget about everything, and everyone, else.

I glance down, my eyes swimming over the words, as I try to figure out what to say. She could be any age, really, ten years younger than my thirty, or even older than me. Her pale skin doesn't give much away, and maybe it's her distinctly aloof vibe that provokes me, makes me ready for the challenge of getting to know her. "Do you have a spare?" I finally ask, and she looks over at me appraisingly. I can already tell she's one of those chicks who will immediately judge me on my appearance, and if I don't pass muster, she won't even respond to my request. I hold my breath as I wait for her answer, because suddenly my whole life is riding on taking a puff of the forbidden, the combination of smoke from her cigarette and my distant memories of puffing away at countless parties, huddled outside my office, letting the glorious taste of tobacco soothe me, rushing back at me making me almost swoon.

Silently, she taps one out and offers it to me and I boldly lean down and take it from the pack with my mouth. I want her to like me, (almost) more than I want her to fuck me—though both would be nice. A lighter appears out of nowhere and she holds the flame to my lips. Maybe the lighter is only for special occasions? I briefly see Bettie Page winking at me as she proffers the flame to the tip of my cig, then I inhale, deeply, loudly, gratefully. I feel the hot smoke fill my lungs, then breathe out, worried I've made a fool of myself, like a teenager overly excited to take her first drag. "Thanks," I say, shutting my eyes for a moment and breathing in through my nose, savoring not just the whiff of tobacco but that feeling of belonging, acceptance, coolness—I'm not just smoking, I'm smoking *with her.*

"No problem. I'm Dana, by the way," she says and sticks out her hand, apparently deeming me acceptable by this point.

"Sam," I say, then wrack my brain trying to think of how to continue this discussion. "I haven't smoked in years, but it's such a beautiful day, and the way you looked so blissful taking a drag made me crave it."

She smiles, then exhales slowly. She inches closer, and soon somehow her smoking has taken on a decidedly erotic overtone. "If you quit, you really shouldn't have that," she says, plucking mine from my fingers and crushing it on the ground with her foot. I watch my little taste of heaven disappear under her big black shoe, not standing a chance against its enemy. I know she's right and am partly thankful for her caring, partly annoyed that she got my hopes up, got my body so keen on the nicotine fix only to snatch it away. But my new crush wasn't about to leave me in the lurch. "Besides, isn't it more fun secondhand?" she says, making the final word sound so tempting I feel my nipples harden. I move even closer, so our thighs are almost touching. I don't care that we are in a very public park

The way her smoky breath lands next to mine as she exhales deliberately onto my skin is enchanting, a high of a whole other sort. My body is tingling with anticipation, arousal, and curiosity. She turns her head away slightly to show off, blowing smoke rings like we're high school kids, and even though I shouldn't be, I'm impressed. We sit there, silently soaking in each other's auras, letting the cloud of smoke woo us just as much as our small talk. Then she pulls out a clove, holding it under my nose and licking the tip suggestively.

"Why don't we go back to my place and smoke this? I live right over there," she says, pointing to a window on Avenue A. I'm not sure which place she means, but it doesn't matter. I'm so intoxicated I'd go anywhere with her. We walk in and are greeted by a cloud of smoke from various substances. "Roommates," she drawls by way of explanation, then drags me into a tiny room painted all in a deep bluish purple that further lulls me under her spell. That's what this feels like—she's a witch (which could be true) and I'm her subject. Some of her iciness has melted under the haze, but she's still not exactly a chatterbox. I don't need her to be, though, and I force myself to close my lips so I don't stare at her slackjawed. She hands me the clove—"hold this"—then proceeds to strip off some layers. I'm not expecting her to be wearing virginal white lace beneath it all, but she is, delicately scalloped panties that hug her tiny ass, a bra that barely covers her nipples. When she bends down to pick up a stray lighter off the floor, I see their pink tips threatening to poke forward, and my mouth waters in a whole new way.

I'm sitting on her futon, and she kneels in her underwear before me, looking totally different from the tough girl I'd encountered in the park. Instead of wanting to slam her against a wall, I want to slowly worship her with my tongue. She leans down, plucking the clove from my fingers with her mouth, her breasts rubbing against my lap as she does. She presses the lighter into my hand, silently asking me to light it, and when I do, she inhales deeply, eyes closed, cheekbones somehow more prominent. I study the stray wisps along her brow, the remnants of dusky gray shadow along her lids, the intense black of her clearly dyed hair. She seems at peace as the sound of her inhalations fills the room, and the sweet smoke she slowly lets pass through her lips warms me as well. I push her hand out of the way and kiss her, letting her pass her smokiness back to me. Her lips are soft, warm, supple, and I seem to melt into them. She'd seemed so hard and closed off outside, but here she's as girlish as one can get, all soft curves, delicate fabrics, the only trace of her edge the crinkling of the clove she keeps in her hand the whole time.

I explore her mouth, swirl my tongue against hers, take over, then slip away just as she's starting to pant. I kiss my way downward, alternately keeping my eyes open and closed, glimpsing her ultra pale skin, then rubbing my cheek against her breast as I undo her bra. I take it off, then bury my head in her cleavage, push her small but perfect tits against my cheeks, revel in the faint hint of sweat and fruit somehow lingering there. I can only measure her response by her breathing, which picks up as I move lower. I glide my tongue over her stomach, down, down, down until I reach the delicate fabric of her panties. I let my tongue toy with the waistband, pulling it back slightly and letting it snap against her, licking along its edges before deciding to leave them on for now. I hold her panties taut as my tongue strokes her wetness, tapping against her clit before I move to suck it between my lips. She's squirming beneath me, lying down on the ground now but still managing to puff, the smoke surrounding us in a haze as I bring her closer and closer. I feel her free hand flail around, trying to grab me, and I twist around so my ass is facing her. She shoves her hand between my legs, clawing at my tights, ripping them facilely as her fingers seek me out, delving into my panties to touch my sex directly. I'm so overwhelmed that I finally push her panties down, straining my head to bend down and around to lick her clit. The more I turn her on, the fiercer her fingers get, and even though she's multitasking, her fingers inside me and her lips wrapped around the dwindling clove, she still knows how to touch me, or maybe I'm so aroused anything would get me off. I don't know how many fingers she has in my pussy or what exactly she's doing, only that it makes me clamp my hands onto her thighs, pushing her legs as far apart as I can as I slam my tongue against her clit, then down to bask in her juices. By the end, when she's got me practically humping her hand, my lips and tongue are sucking her clit like my life depended on it. I bury my face there to get her off, but also because I almost cannot handle the pleasure she wreaks out of me, so calmly, so easily. I come in a silent explosion, offering her the aftermath of my orgasm as my fingers probe her sex while I try to make her clit even bigger. I hear something sizzle, but don't turn around as I rev up my pace until she's twitching beneath me, a small stream of liquid sliding along my fingers.

When I finally sit up, the smoke lingering in the air even as all I taste is her, I see a small hole burned into her carpet where she's smashed the nub of her smoke into the ground, but she doesn't seem to mind.

"Wow," she says shakily, laughing even as her eyes attempt to read mine, while I do the same. Then she does the only logical thing, patting around for another smoke. This time, she offers me one, too, and I accept.

HOT WAX

ALISON DUBOIS

SATURDAY IS MY FAVORITE day of the week. Usually it means sloth and rest and relaxation, things I can appreciate! I like waking to the smell of freshly brewed coffee and baking cinnamon rolls wafting through the house or gently being stirred awake for great sex. No matter how you slice it, wonderfully appealing to one's senses!

This Saturday began as so many others… I opened my eyes hearing the sound of water. The shower was going. It explained why Anne had abandoned our warm bed. It was early yet, darkness still clinging to the day.

Pressing my ear to the door I heard singing, it made

me smile. Anne loved to sing, and singing in the shower was one of her favorite stages. But I had an entirely different audience in mind for this morning.

I opened the door stealthily, her backside a tantalizing blur behind the dolphin-print curtain. For a moment I stood just watching her wash. The careful and deliberate way she guided the bar of soap in her hand over the natural curve of her shoulders, across the peaks of her breasts and down to her tangled mass of blonde curls, gave me chills. It was time. I let my robe drop and eased in behind her.

Under the steady stream of hot water I pulled her against me. At first she jumped, but then she laughed. Immediately she pivoted around locking me in a long, juicy kiss.

Suddenly I felt her lathering my bush with a gob of soap and suds, teasing my clit as her fingers slid along the ridge of my woman-lips. I groaned cocking my head back and leaning against the shower stall. I lifted one leg and rested my foot on the lip of the bath.

She directed the spray of water down my pelvis as an insistent stream flowed over my cunt. Then she knelt between my legs and began to massage my mound with her tongue, the water still pouring over me like a mini waterfall. The blend of soft strokes from her tongue combined with the rock-salt water on my clit, made me feel heady.

Then she pushed two fingers in my hole. Automatically my legs started shaking, my hips rocking. The longer she pumped my pussy, the closer I could feel myself climbing to that familiar jubilant peak. My bead was hard and aching for release but her feather caresses were too light to bring me to a finish, so I guided her head more firmly against my throbbing rosebud. She understood and in unison began sucking me just as four fingers went inside.

I heard myself growling and grunting as I fucked her face and her fingers. By now my whole body was straining, growing tight, ready for release.

Slowly I felt the tail of an intrinsic kite pulling me along, farther and farther into the wild blue yonder as I screamed her name in defiance and spasmed in her arms. She scrambled to steady me, help me regain my balance. Not an easy thing to do with flowing water and suds!

"Ohhhhh, Anne Marie!" I heard myself cry out as I drew her into my arms and started kissing and licking her face. Instantly my tongue pushed into her mouth. I had to have her! Our tongues sublimely screwing with our senses. Now it was my turn to explore her as I plunged fingers into her woman cavern.

Immediately Anne began fucking my hand with force, moaning and clinging to me desperately, building herself, searching for her own utopia. She'd thrust forward as I'd shove back, our unabashed utterances of heat melded into one uniform plea of passion.

With my free hand I pinched her clit. Instantly she began to buck again, writhing in delight. Then she started kissing me so fiercely I could hardly breathe. I knew her well enough by now to know what *those* kisses meant.

This was the weekend and Anne was definitely *in the*

mood, which meant she wanted me to royally screw her brains out. Something I was only too willing to comply with. I found her supremely sexy when she was like this and loved every minute of it. It was what I lived for. Building her up, taking her over the top, devouring her pussy...had become a fine art. I loved leaving my scent on her as much as I loved having her scent on me. It made me feel so intricately connected to her. There just isn't anything as enticing as the scent of a woman aroused.

By the time we staggered to the bed we crashed haphazardly on the mattress, so intertwined with each other that we scarcely felt the tumble. Instantly I rolled her on her back, spread her legs and began eating her tender meat for all I was worth. Her bush's curls were so soft after the shower they tickled my face as I munched her.

But it was her clit that had me engrossed. It was a purplish-red, engorged and rigid. I continued to tease and taunt her, nibbling lightly at first, then more insistent. She let me know in no uncertain terms what she wanted, as her hands pressed my head against her taut pearl.

I wouldn't keep her waiting. She was a woman after my own heart, passionate and sensual. Making love had become as integral to us as breathing. We delighted in exploring each other, delighted in new experiences and fulfilling any desire or fantasy we dared to imagine. We were two bands of a tightly woven chord. In fact, Anne was the only woman in over twenty years and numerous partners that truly understood me sexually. Understood without question, my primal need and how intimately it was connected to my being, my feelings of love. You could say that sex was very nearly sacred to me. She more than understood, she shared my base but ethereal need.

Weekends like this were the ultimate high for us so I indulged myself with absolute abandon. There wasn't anything I wouldn't do or try. I liked it all, digital, oral, mutual, toys…exploring. Whatever floated her boat would most certainly float mine just from the sheer passion it evoked.

No sooner had I finished swallowing her come when she sat up to fetch a vibrating dildo from a collection we kept in the top drawer of the nightstand. Her eyes said it all: she was laughing, awaiting my response. I chuckled.

Her choice was one of the larger purple ones we owned, it was soft and malleable. She smeared lubricant all over the tip and shaft. In return, I assumed the position on my hands and knees, waiting… I felt her pushing the toy in slowly, gently pacing me with even thrusts until I became lost in the rhythm. Aware of nothing but each penetrating stroke propelling me farther and farther into the cosmos.

"Like that do ya?" she taunted. All I could do was grunt in response. "Maybe I ought to stop—" she waited, her hand abruptly stopped, holding the dildo. I looked over my shoulder–suddenly my utopia seemed a million miles away.

"Please, I pleaded in a whisper.

Anne's smile was full of mischief. She knew me so well and knew that just the threat of delaying pleasure would unravel me.

"Tell me how much you need it?" she continued her game.

"Honey—" I begged.

"Tell me. Tell me what a naughty girl like you needs, hmm?" she stood up starting to move away.

Was she serious? I was speechless. Over the years she and I had certainly participated in our share of games and seductions with the intent to keep things "fresh" between us. But rarely did Anne refuse me. And rarer still was this side: flexing her muscle. It daunted me. Had I not needed her so much at the moment, I probably would have analyzed why she was doing it or gotten really pissed. Instead my suspended fruition was only making me anxious.

"Lady, are you trying to drive me nuts or what?" I said half jokingly, still hoping to keep the mood light and return to the wonderful fervor we'd been engaged in. Her green eyes stared at me. They were emerald lightning bolts piercing my soul. This was a side of her I had little experience with.

Inexplicably as if she'd had a change of heart she slowly reinserted the toy, with her free hand beginning to trail feather caresses over my hips, back, and legs. I felt her lips kiss over the plane of my back. I was soaking up the tender touches until she abruptly bit me.

"Ouch!" I squealed. Simultaneously we stopped. I stared at her. Her eyes were fiery demons staring back at me. For the first time a wave of fear swept over me. I wasn't sure I liked where this was going. But yet a part of me was intrigued.

"Trust me?" she asked.

I rolled onto my back, looking up at her. My mind was spinning. What did she mean? Trust her with what? For the first time I began to wonder what she *really* wanted.

"Yes—" I said a little pensive. We'd been together for four years and our life and loving together had always been good between us. That had to count for something, didn't it? My mind flashed back to many moments, suddenly joined together in my collective memory.

Out of the blue she slapped my ass. It was sharp and stung. I moved away from her laughing eyes.

"I love it!" she exclaimed. Then she disappeared from the bedroom.

What was she up to? I could hear her rattling around in the kitchen. It made me curious and nervous…Would I like it? Could I tell her no if I didn't?

Finally she returned with a rather thick blue candle. Was she planning on fucking me with it? We'd tried a number of things before but a candle being so brittle and wide, didn't appeal to me. I looked at it and looked into her eyes. She smiled back with that same devil-may-care attitude.

"Wha—?" I gestured toward the candle.

"Be patient!" she scolded before she lit it. I gasped. Fire? My mind was reeling. This wasn't looking good. I wasn't into pain….

"Wait!" I put my hand up. Her focus shifted to me as she set the burning candle on a saucer. I watched the flame flickering…then I looked at her. Her eyes met mine with a hunger I'd never seen.

"Are you ready?"

"For what?" I squawked.

"For something new, baby?"

"That depends—" I curled my knees under me.

"Ally...come on. Trust me."

"I don't like that look in your eyes," I confessed.

"Baby, I love you. It won't hurt...much," she finished in a whisper. It was the only word I heard. *It won't hurt much.* What the hell did that mean? And why was it the server of such pain was always the one to make such declarations?

"Then why don't we do you first?" I opted for the coward's way out.

"How can we do that when you don't know what I have in mind? Besides, I *do* want you to do it to me, but first things first... *Trust* me," she said again. "Lay back," she instructed. Cautiously I obliged.

I watched her grab the candle. Instinctively I started to hedge and draw up, away from her, but Anne pressed her hand against my midriff and pinned me, prone.

Carefully she tipped the candle to allow small droplets of hot wax to spill on my skin. The first bead burned, leaving a light red circle around the cooling wax. I gasped. My mind hissed: could I do this? In increments Anne began making her way south. When she got to my hairline, my legs sharply slapped closed. Impatiently she glowered, waiting for me to play.

"That'll hurt," I whimpered, trying to plead my case.

"Only for a second, but it'll make your clit hard and stimulated," she promised.

"How do you know? I thought you said you hadn't tried this," I reminded her.

"It doesn't mean I haven't read about it....Besides, I

promise you, I'll make it worth your while." It was that statement that made me surrender. Knowing Anne's word was good.

I forced myself to lie splayed, inviting the hot wax into my wet, aching loins. Anne's smile enveloped her whole face. I'd never seen her so delighted. She moved with a deliberate and calculated maneuver as she began to tip the candle.

"Honey, open yourself more." She instructed. I hesitated, still afraid of the consequences should her little experiment not work. "Go on!" she snapped angrily as a vein of hot wax spilled over her fingers. Telling myself over and over again that a good relationship means having trust in one another, I finally gave in.

I wanted to close my eyes but I couldn't. I had to watch the hot transparent liquid tumbling in space until a bead of it hit just above my clitoris. It burned.

"Ow!" I recoiled.

"Stay!" she demanded, pouring more into my secret place, making a lavender-scented mold.

"Oh…" I jerked, pulling my hands away. As if that was her cue, immediately Anne returned the candle to the saucer and was upon me. Kissing me and stroking me everywhere but on my pussy, until at last she nuzzled her face into my slit and with her tongue worked over the wax that covered my woman bead like a sheath. Her tongue made the wax soft and malleable again.

Damn but she was right! Each time her tongue slid over me, it would send wonderful reverberating circles of pleasure spreading all through me. Before I knew it, I was on the verge of coming.

"Oh honey...I'm losing it—" I heard myself whine. Suddenly I was back in her arms, being tenderly rocked by my woman. I found myself smiling.

"Look—" She displayed a light blue mold of my genitals. She placed it on the nightstand.

"Ready?" I asked her. She chuckled sprawling out beside me. Spice was nice.

I clutched the candle...

THE BREAK
CHERYL B

MY EX-GIRLFRIEND KATE INVITED me over for dinner. The minute she opened the door I was immediately reminded of what attracted me to her from the beginning; the blue eyes, dark spiky hair, small sturdy body, and the perfectly round bottom covered in baggy jeans. I wanted to turn her around and smack her ass but we hadn't seen each other in over two months and had more pressing things to get over first.

After the awkward "Hello" hug, we sat down at her kitchen table for the lasagna, which she had baked to perfection and served with a crisp salad and warm bread.

I'd almost forgotten what a good cook she was—almost forgotten that on our first date, Kate had described herself as a domestic butch. "I like to cook," she had said. "And I like to eat," I answered before pushing her down on the bed.

When we were finished with the lasagna, we moved into the living room where we sat on separate parts of her sectional couch to watch the DVD. It doesn't matter what the movie was and I can't remember it one bit. But I found myself trying to figure out a way to smoothly move myself onto her section of the couch. Maybe if I stretched out far enough, I would touch her leg. I tried this several times, but couldn't completely work it. The last time I sat on this couch with her, she lay across my knee as I smacked her fleshy cheeks with a paddle. I'd worked it into a good rhythm, moving from one red-welted cheek to another with an intensity that almost scared me.

"Baby, I don't think I can take any more," Kate cried.

"Oh, you're going to take it." I picked up the rhythm.

"It feels so good," she acquiesced.

"I bet it does." I continued smacking.

But that night I kept my distance as she didn't seem too interested in crossing over onto my area of the couch.

Following the movie, we stood in her doorway for the good-bye.

"It's late," I said looking at the clock on the wall.

"What do you mean by that?" she asked cautiously.

I reached out and touched her hand—I couldn't help myself. When she touched me back, it was obvious we were both under the spell of the familiar.

"I mean it's past midnight," I offered.

"Does that mean you want to stay over?" Kate asked.

"Do you want me to?"

"If you want to."

"Are you sure?"

"Yeah, it's too late. The bus is weird now."

"I can sleep on the couch."

"You don't have to do that."

"Are you sure?"

"Yes."

Kate handed me my favorite red flannel pajamas. The ones I'd always worn when I stayed over during our two year relationship. They were soft and warm and as soon as they were in my hands, I realized how much I'd missed them. Or perhaps I'd just missed her. I went into the bathroom to change. Just a few months prior, I would have disrobed right in the middle of the living room, but since we were broken up I felt self-conscious. I was surprised that she had even kept the pajamas; I was even more surprised to find my pink toothbrush waiting for me in her medicine cabinet in the same spot I had always kept it. But then her toothbrush was still in my cabinet too. I didn't want to throw it out. "Lesbian couples never really break up," someone said to me years ago, "they just find new ways to be codependent." I never thought that was true. I'm not one of those people who could be friends with my exes so this was new territory for me.

Kate's new girl made her presence known in the bathroom as well. There was an unfamiliar hair product sitting out on the sink next to expensive loose powder.

On the shelf above were two tacky hair accessories with long strands of blonde hair still attached. I picked up one of the barrettes and studied the specimen. I could tell by the way the hair caught the light that the other girl was a natural blonde. Kate always told me she didn't like blondes; she only liked brunettes, like me. My ex-boy-friend told me he didn't like women with large breasts, he only liked women with smaller chests, like me. You can imagine where that went when we broke up.

By the time I got ready, Kate was already in bed, tucked up to her chin, journal in hand. I didn't know what to expect. Was this really just a friendly sleepover? Were we going to get it on? Even worse, I didn't know what I wanted to have happen. I got into the bed and she stopped writing, ending the entry with an exaggerated flourish of her pen. She put the journal on her nightstand and I realized that I'd never seen her write in a journal before. Was this a new thing? *So much can happen in two months*, I thought as I ducked down under the covers.

She shut off the light and moved closer to me, placing her arm around my waist. I didn't know whether to burst out crying or kiss her desperately. Either way, the weight of our separation was apparent and we melted into each other as if nothing had happened, as if we'd never broken up.

I rolled on top of her and held down her arms. She was my prisoner.

"I'm your prisoner," Kate said playfully.

"Oh, yes you are," I reached over the side of her bed and felt around for her wrist restraints. They were still attached to the bed frame, one on each side. It was nice to see my girl hadn't lost her lust for pervery. I turned her around, belly down, bottom up, and tightly fastened each wrist.

"Stick your pretty ass in the air," I whispered in her ear.

She did as I told her, pushing her ass out in exaggeration. I pulled her satin blindfold off the bedpost, fastened it around her head.

"Oh no!" she cried.

I opened the bottom drawer of her nightstand, where she kept the supplies and felt around for her riding crop. It was at the bottom. Did this mean she hadn't used it in a while? Was blondie not into spanking?

I spread her knees farther apart and fastened each ankle in its restraint.

"Don't move," I told her and smacked her ass hard with my hand just to emphasize the seriousness of the situation.

"Yes," she answered.

"Yes, what?"

"Yes, Ma'am," she answered. This was all part of our game and I was ecstatic to hear that she hadn't forgotten the dialogue.

Then I picked up the riding crop, got off the bed, and walked a few feet back to regard the situation; my little domestic butch prisoner was waving her ample ass in the air just waiting for it. No one else had ever done this to me: turned me into such a dirty foul-mouthed bitch with a bad attitude and a steady, sadistic hand. Before

Kate I was not particularly interested in much outside the typical fucking and sucking that had been part of my existence as a bisexual woman. But something about her just brought out my femme top.

She was really begging for it now, waving her bottom in the air.

"You better smack my ass soon, or else," she implored, barely able to move any part of her body except her ass which was thrusting wildly. I could see her pussy slick and glistening from behind.

"Or else what?" I laughed, my own juices bubbling over inside my panties. "What are you going to do to me, you're all tied up."

"I'll smack *your* ass," she said defiantly. She knew that was never going to happen.

"You're going to smack my ass?"

"Yes, I'm going to smack your ass if you don't start smacking mine. Please, please don't make me wait any longer."

I stepped closer to the bed. She whimpered in anticipation. I ran my implement across her cheeks, down her crack, and separated her soaking wet lips with the tip of the riding crop. She began to tremble all over, practically falling over on one side, her ass falling toward the bed.

"Get up. Put your ass back in the air," I said lightly smacking her bottom with the palm of my hand.

"Yes, Ma'am!" she said. She was shaking but she got back up and once again assumed the position.

I continued to play with her pussy lips and rub her clit with the riding crop. The black leather skated easily over the deep red folds of wet flesh. I wanted to reach down and taste her but managed to focus on the task at hand. I backed away, raised my arm over my head, and brought the riding crop down on the fleshy bosom of her left butt cheek. She gasped, then moaned.

I watched as the skin rose forming a perfect red welt. I raised my arm even farther above and came down on the right side. I thought about the blonde, leaving her hair all over the place and staking her claim in the bathroom. I imagined her paws all over Kate—the bitch had probably even worn my pajamas! My favorite pajamas! I bore down on Kate's ass with a fierce velocity.

With each break on her ass, I thought about "The Break" we had taken in our relationship. *What a brilliant idea that was!* I thought. "Breaks" never work out; they're just ways to belabor the "Breaking Up" process, throw another wrench into the already gut-wrenching mix, which then just spins around and hits you in the head. I notice a long blonde hair on the sheet by Kate's knee and I am filled with an incredible sadness. I thought about the guy I'd been with since "The Break"—as bland as a bowl of vanilla ice cream and even less satisfying —no one will ever bring out his inner pervert. He has no inner pervert, some people are just like that and you have to accept it. But I keep going back because I don't know what else to do. It's hard to meet people in this city and I've never been one to be alone.

I'd heard from a good friend that Kate was crazy about the blonde and as I stood there lovingly beating her ass to a fuchsia-tinted pulp, I was filled with an incredible sadness. And I somehow knew, that no matter how much we wanted each other that night, we would never be together again. When Kate yelled for me to stop, I collapsed on top of her, both of us crying like we did when we first fell in love. Her ass was warm against the front of my flannel pajamas and we both fell facedown on a bed that could no longer contain us.

PAINTING THE MUSE

KRISTINA WRIGHT

WHAT FIRST CAUGHT MY attention were her hands. Her hands, with their long, pale fingers and short, buffed nails. Her hands stroked me and with her touch, she memorized me. With her hands, she turned me on, got me wet, got me off. Annabella's hands. Her strong, beautiful hands teased my fevered imagination long after her scent faded from the air around me and her laughter was just a memory.

Annabella was an artist struggling to put together a gallery show while teaching art classes to students with a fraction of her talent. I met her through a life drawing class at the University of Chicago. I'm not an artist, I'm an actress. Correction: I'm a waitress aspiring to be an actress who does some modeling for extra cash. Modeling for an art class means stripping down to my birthday suit. There are worse ways to make a living and I didn't have to worry about the art students pawing me.

It's a good gig, being a nude model. Good pay, good atmosphere.

I'm not particularly modest, so it doesn't phase me to be the only naked body in the room. Granted, it can get a little tedious sometimes having to hold the same pose for an hour or more, but I have an active imagination. I keep myself entertained by practicing my monologue for auditions or, rarely, running lines for whatever theater production I'm currently in.

Annabella's class was composed of about a dozen students of varying ages, most of them edging closer to the retirement scene than the club scene. They were all respectful, almost deferential, of Annabella. On the other hand, they seemed positively terrified of me, as if I had an explosive device strapped to my thigh. They spoke to me haltingly when I was naked and they weren't much more comfortable with me when I was clothed. That was okay with me, I wasn't there to make friends.

The only one who would meet my eyes when I was naked was Annabella, but that had as much to do with her own self-confidence as it did her familiarity with models. She had long, blonde hair and delicate, patrician features. Her body was lean and angular, functional more than graceful—much like her hands. She wasn't the type of woman I was normally attracted to, actually. She seemed aloof, untouchable. Ice princess is the phrase that came to mind when I thought of her. I was the one who was uncomfortable, especially when I was naked.

I was surprised when she asked me to stay after class one evening. The ninety-minute art lesson left me exhausted and stiff and I longed for a hot bath and my warm bed. Still, Annabella's request felt more like a command and I nodded tiredly in agreement.

"Just let me get dressed," I said, tying the belt of my robe as I padded toward the workroom where I stored my clothes during class.

"Could you wait?" she asked. "It won't take long. I want to show you something."

I sighed. "Sure."

"Wait here."

I sat on one of the student's stools, twisting my neck to crack it. The room was chillier than usual, probably because no one had thought yet to turn on the heat. It was late September already, but we had been in the grips of a very pleasant Indian summer for weeks and no one was in a hurry to welcome winter. Still, I'd have to say something to Annabella so I wouldn't have to suffer through the next week's session. My nipples were like rocks, poking through my thin robe like some 1950s pinup and aching like they'd been pinched and twisted all night.

Annabella returned finally, carrying a medium-sized canvas. She had it facing her, so I couldn't see what was on it. Despite my exhaustion, I was curious. I wondered if it was something she was working on. She put it up on one of the students' easels, but it wasn't until she stepped to the side that I could get a clear view of it.

It was a painting of me, though I didn't realize it at first. Art is a visceral experience, much more so than photography. I responded to the art at first, not to the subject. What I saw were the soft, rounded curves of a woman, her pale body stretched out on an ornate purple couch, long red hair trailing down one shoulder, and a playful smile that made me want to smile. The light of the painting was ethereal, as if the woman—which I finally realized was me—cast the glow that lit the space around her. It wasn't quite an angelic effect, because the woman so obviously reveled in her nakedness. I realized the luminosity was not light but eroticism, as if all her passion was bottled up, trapped beneath the surface, ready to burst from the painting. It was, to say the least, a powerful effect.

It wasn't until I took a deep breath that I realized I'd been holding it in since she'd revealed the painting to me.

"Well?" she asked, sounding wholly unlike herself. "What do you think?"

I was moved by her art, but I was even more touched by the tentativeness in her voice, the realization that she was nervous about my reaction and eager for my approval. This was not the Annabella I knew, but I liked her.

"It's incredible, Annabella. I'm honored," I said. "I

hope it doesn't sound vain to say that it's one of your most beautiful paintings."

She laughed, regaining some of her confidence. "It is vain, but that's all right. You deserve a little vanity." I couldn't stop looking at the painting, at myself. Was that how she saw me? Was I that beautiful, erotic creature? I didn't feel like that. I had taken enough acting classes to know I would never pass for the ingénue or even the leading lady. I was a character actress, the full-figured best friend, the secondary character who added color and dimension to the plot—and I was fine with that. But Annabella had made me into—painted me into—a seductress, an erotic beauty.

"Why?" I couldn't quite figure out how to phrase the question. I didn't know if she would understand. I tried again. "Why like that?"

She looked from me to the painting and then back to me. "Because you are so incredibly beautiful and you don't even know it."

It was trite, clichéd. Simple. Yet, I believed her. "Thank you."

I took a step toward her, wanting somehow to let her know how grateful I was that she would not only paint me, but let me be the first to see it. I put my hand on her shoulder, felt the fine bones shift beneath my hand as I leaned forward and kissed her cheek.

"Thank you so much, Annabella." When I started to move away, she put her hand on my waist, stilling me. She leaned in, as if to kiss my cheek, but her lips settled against mine. They were cold, from the air or from nervousness, I couldn't be sure. Our lips and her hand on my waist were the only parts of our body that touched. As I relaxed into the kiss and felt her lips part and her tongue tentatively lick my bottom lip, I realized I wanted to touch more of her. I put my arms around her narrow waist and pulled her closer, feeling strong and protective of the thin, delicate creature in my arms.

She let out a soft, breathy sigh against my mouth as if, finally, she could relax. "I have wanted to kiss you since that first night in class," she confessed. "I've been a woman obsessed."

Her confession, her raw vulnerability, made me ache. I kissed her again, taking her bottom lip into my mouth and sucking it with gentle persistence. She pulled me closer, molding her thin body against my fuller one, stroking my hip with one hand while she twisted my long hair with her other hand.

"So beautiful," she murmured against my mouth. "So luscious." I whimpered as she trailed kisses across my jaw and down my neck. I clung to her, not sure who was supporting whom, as we sunk to the hardwood floor in one slow, fluid motion. Annabella was stretched out on top of me, her warm body between my legs, the cold, hard floor against my back.

She knelt up between my spread thighs and undid the belt of my robe. I trembled as she parted it, feeling shy and vulnerable, as if she had never seen me naked before. In a way, Annabella had seen more of me than anyone ever had.

She leaned forward, running her hands down my

body, pausing to stroke my hard nipples before running the flat of her hand over my stomach, down farther over my mound. I spread my legs wider, opening myself fully to her as she touched me. I could feel the wetness growing, could almost imagine my cunt swelling and opening for her.

"You are stunning," she said, her gaze between my legs. She slid a finger gently inside me, then pulled it out and over my clit. I gasped and she chuckled. "I can't believe you're here, like this."

She stretched out on top of me again, shifting her weight so that her legs were spread on either side of my right leg while her hand worked between my thighs. She wore thin cotton pants and a simple white linen blouse and her body was warm, far warmer than the room warranted. I put my hands on the back of her head and pulled her down so I could kiss her mouth while she slid her finger back inside me. She caressed me lightly, as if learning my internal curves the same way she had memorized my external ones.

I thrust my hips up to meet that one slender finger, longing for more. She gasped as my thigh pressed up hard between her legs. I wrapped my arm around her waist and held her as she rocked against me. She added a second finger and I gasped.

"Oh, God. You're driving me crazy." I pressed my mouth against her neck and bit down, gently at first and then harder as her fingers became more insistent.

She didn't answer, she only continued to fuck me, driving her fingers deep into my cunt and then withdrawing them before pushing them into me once more. I braced my feet against the floor to keep us from sliding, my robe riding up underneath me. I thrust my thigh against her cunt hard so she could feel some of what I was feeling.

She kept fucking me, slowly, steadily– those two fingers making me throb inside for something else.

"More, Annabella," I whimpered. "More, please."

She added a third finger, slowly twisting them inside me like a corkscrew in a wine bottle, capturing me on her hand. I writhed against her as I cried out, my voice echoing off the walls. She added her cries to mine as she rode my thigh, driving her pelvic bone down onto my soft, bare flesh. I knew I would be bruised for the experience, but it didn't matter. If anything, it only aroused me more to think of having Annabella's mark on my body.

"Fuck me," I cried, my voice a plaintive plea.

She turned her hand, getting four fingers into me, opening me, spreading my engorged cunt. I felt stretched, open, exposed. I ground my clit against the palm of her hand, whimpering as she fucked me. Shifting her weight, she braced herself on her knees so she could touch my body with her other hand. I reached between her legs and pressed against the wet crotch of her pants, feeling the stiff ridge of her clit. I rubbed it hard, harder, until she cried out and pinched and rolled one of my nipples between her fingers.

"More?" she asked, barely a whisper.

I nodded.

She asked again, more insistently, "More?"

"Please, Annabella, more."

She withdrew her fingers almost all the way and then she was pushing them back into me. Out, then in. Out again, then in, only more, fuller, deeper, her thumb added, widening me, opening me, pushing me farther than I had ever been pushed. So full, so swollen. I groaned, shaking my head back and forth on the floor, my hair making a swishing sound on the hardwood.

"No?" She made as if to pull away.

I reached down and gripped her wrist. "Yes!" I moaned through gritted teeth. "Yes!"

She let me guide her hand. I blinked away tears of emotion, but there was no pain. Only fullness. Completeness. A wholeness I'd never felt before.

"Fuck me, Annabella," I whispered. "Please."

She did. She pushed into me, rocking her entire body on me, riding my hand between her legs while I took her hand inside my body. Slowly, slowly, so slow I thought I would die from the excruciating need, she fucked me. Her fist felt like a large, hard knot inside me, filling a void I hadn't known was there. I tilted my hips, felt something give way inside me and then her hand simply seemed to melt into my body, as if she had always been there.

I felt her tense, felt the quiver in her taut thigh muscles as I rubbed her clit through her pants until she came. She went rigid above me, her hand still inside me. She tilted her head back and moaned, coming as I rolled her clit between my fingers. The thin fabric of her pants was damp from her arousal. I palmed her cunt and squeezed as if I could wring from her the wetness she had coaxed from me.

She leaned forward and collapsed on top of me, her wrist pressing up against my clit while her hand pushed down into my body, causing an uncomfortable sensation of fullness. It was the closest thing to pain I'd felt since she'd started. Just as I was about to ask her to take her hand away, she straightened her arm and rocked her hand inside me. Over and over, she moved her hand until the sensation felt like vibrations traveling through my body. I bit my lip to keep from screaming.

"Look up," she said. "Look!"

I was nearly incoherent, so close to orgasm I felt as if my muscles had turned to liquid and was leaking out from between my legs. I did as she said, looked up and over her shoulder. I saw myself looking down from her painting, saw the knowing smile, the light illuminating not just the painting but also our bodies on the floor. I saw myself the way Annabella saw me, I saw the passion, the eroticism. And then I came.

I arched my hips off the floor until the only thing supporting my and Annabella's weight were my shoulders and feet pressed to the floor. I came on her hand, feeling the sweet agony of being more full, more engorged than I had ever been. I came, screaming her name over and over in a litany of desire even while I stared into my own eyes in the painting she had created of me. *For* me.

"Beautiful girl," she murmured, her hand still inside me. I'm not sure she could have pulled away if she had wanted to, my body had clamped down on her, refusing her exit. "Beautiful, beautiful muse."

We lay there kissing and laughing in a tangle of limbs and clothing and hair and sweat, her fist still inside my slick, swollen cunt.

Above us, I smiled.

STRAIGHT GIRLS ARE EASY

ROXANNE YORK

SHE'S STRAIGHT. STRAIGHT STRAIGHT STRAIGHT.
The thought, a truthful observation pumped into my head by my friends and my overactive brain, pounds through my skull even as my entire body itches with the thought of getting my hands on her. Yes, she's straight, but she's not the prissy kind of straight girl who spends hours getting her ponytail and lip gloss just right, the kind who'd sooner kiss a wizened troll of a man than another girl. She's the kind of straight girl who's smart, boho, hot without trying, the kind who thinks twice about letting her hair down, who prefers wine and burgers over girlie

99

cocktails and steaks. She's naturally small, petite but not dainty, and usually wears soft, see-through white T-shirts and jeans that cling to her ass perfectly. I'm much femmier than she'll ever be, but that just makes this agonizing crush all the more confusing.

I've decided that tonight's the night. It's been months and all I've done is stare at her from across the room, or up close as her intense eyes stare back at me with something that might be lust but is definitely interest. I take in the way her brows are perfectly sculpted, smooth, long arches over those wide brown eyes, the way her smile catches me off guard, small and shy and unexpected. We're in one of a million crowded bars we rotate through, usually with friends. It's a rare night alone but I've trouble focusing on her words, too busy figuring out what to say, how to approach her for that first, vital kiss. I've let my mind get totally carried away, so it takes me by surprise when she's the one to lean toward me first, her lips soft but firm. I let out a little breath, right into her mouth, as her tongue tentatively seeks out mine. My whole body tingles, little shivers of anticipation as our legs touch, mine bare, hers denim-covered but just as warm. None of the awkwardness I'd expected is there; it's just those brief getting-to-know-you brushes of our tongues. Maybe all my worries have been for naught, but suddenly none of that matters as I close my eyes and lose myself in the feeling, still seeing her deep, intense eyes on mine, torn between grabbing her for more and stilling time so we can kiss forever. I lightly touch her hair, which seems longer than it should be, the soft ends trailing down to her shoulders.

We stare at each other, deep and intense, trying to read minds as our fingers dart lightly over our fuzzy arms, asking questions as surely as if our mouths were moving. We answer, haltingly, but there's no turning back now. After what feels like an eternity, we somehow separate and make our way to my place as if in a trance. We don't speak, each of us afraid to break the magical spell. But that would be impossible at this point, and, straight or not, she slips easily into my bed.

With her arms above her head as she lies on her back, I look her up and down, not even sure where to start. I nudge her legs apart, sliding my knee against the warmth I find there, grinding it, hard, against her pussy while she lifts herself up to reach me. We struggle like that, me pressing down against her while she arches up to reach me until I lean down, grabbing her wrists and easily holding them down on the bed. For once, I'm grateful for being bigger, for that added bit of strength that allows me to overpower her, and I sense that she is too. I lean down so our lips are almost touching, but instead of kissing again, I bite her lower lip, getting my makeup all over her as I suckle, my knee continuing to press against her increasingly damp jeans. When I do finally touch her as I've been dreaming about, I want her slick and creamy, wetter for me than she's ever been for anyone else. I tickle her arm with my nails, lightly scraping them along the sensitive skin of the inside of her wrist before pushing my tongue inside her mouth.

Finally, I turn her over. "Stay," I tell her, the command

lingering in the room, setting the stage for the entire rest of our encounter, because she does. I lift her shirt to reveal her small, thin back, and lick a line up her spine, peeling the shirt off as I go until it's time to lift it over her shoulders. She's not wearing a bra, and my hands reach underneath her, easily covering her small breasts, the nipples beaded, pressing into the mattress. I'm getting hot and sticky, my temperature rising as I'm filled with that always uncontrollable, utterly consuming need to have her, take her, hold her—whoever she happens to be. Put me in a room with a half-naked beautiful girl and my mind goes blank, my body simply going on instinct as I devour her. She's so thin I can feel every move she makes, can lie on top of her and feel her contort, getting off on making her squirm. My tongue licks along her back while my hands cup her tits, holding them while I marvel at how they fit perfectly in my palms like they simply belong there and always have. I bite her back, lightly, my teeth sinking into her taut, salty skin, and she moans. It's a small sound, but I can tell I've hit a jackpot of sorts. I tug on both nipples at once, and she arches her back up, pulling them even farther. I press them hard, twisting, my face buried in the small of her back, the glinting traces of glitter from my long-ago gloss now lost, mixed within the sheen of her sweat and arousal. She kicks, her denim-covered leg rising up and slamming back down on the bed, and I twist harder, dig into her, a battle of wills that's really not a battle at all, yet one we keep fighting, growling, snarling, pushing, pulling. I let go of one nipple and bring my hand to her back, scraping my polished purple nails down her tender flesh, letting the sharpness leave red streaks along her pale skin even as I slam my knee hard against her cunt.

I pinch the delicate skin at the back of her neck and she yelps, then growls, then sighs. I twist my fingers through her thin hair, turn her head slightly so I can see her. Her brow is sweaty, messy, and tears seem to glint along the edges of her eye. I briefly wonder whether she's ever done this before—not fuck another girl, but let herself go, get entirely lost in her own desire. Her eyes are far away, floating, as she blinks them, struggling to focus on me even as I trail both my hands along her skin, pinching, pressing anywhere that seems like a good spot to settle. Her thin body looks even smaller unclothed, yet there are vast expanses along her back, wide swaths of smooth white skin that I need to touch. Whether she needs me to touch them as well is open for debate, but I've come this far and I must find out.

This is the farthest thing from casual as you can get. Casual doesn't make your heart pound so hard you're worried you might have to call a doctor, casual doesn't make you gasp every time she moves, wiggling that pert little ass without even meaning to, casual doesn't make tears start to form, deep in your soul, when she hisses out your name between her teeth, in a tone of voice you've never heard her use before, not even at her angriest. I sink my teeth into her shoulder blade, not getting too far before I hit hardness beneath, but it's as satisfying as any vampire's feast. I edge my fingers under her thin hair, let them tangle there in a way that'll make them hard to remove. I tug, hard, and bite again, fingers and teeth together making her eyes shut and another glorious hiss emerge. I lift my head, and turning her over, cover her face with soft kisses that speak nothing of my desire to press my way inside her, to feel her everywhere, to press my fingers into her until they can't go any farther. My lips are light as a feather as they bounce along from her eyelids to her nose, cheeks, and mouth. When I open my own eyes to see her face so sleek, so smooth, so trusting, I melt once again, in an altogether different way. She opens her hazel eyes, and they seem clearer than they usually are, less murky, combining umpteen colors into one sharp and clear green. They meet my brown ones for several seconds, our gazes steady, direct, sure.

I lie on top of her once again and gently kiss my way along her gorgeous face. Now I want her in a whole new way, the desire rising up from somewhere deeper than my pussy, somewhere that might make me cry too. It's not enough to just have her in my bed anymore, that alone is not the prize I've been searching for, though as her ass trembles just slightly, a small signal to let me know that she too wants this, I'm aware that her presence is a prize. But suddenly, faced with her quivering frame, I realize I'm utterly unprepared. Not in the usual ways; I have half a dozen bottles of lube, a drawerful of toys, a kinky treasure trove we could spend hours exploring. What I'm not ready for is the difference between fantasy and reality, and how the latter truly does rock my world as my fingers seek out her lips, her breasts, her everything. When she does the same to me, two tentative fingers pleading with me to enter, running along my slit until I tug them inside, I feel the tears trickle down my eyes. Not tears of sadness per se, but not exactly joy either. She keeps herself inside me while reaching up to wipe them away, and suddenly, they're gone, and I'm back, fully focused on her. "Beautiful," I say softly, both a description of her visage and her touch, and she seems to perk up at my encouragement, bending her fingers to properly bring me to where I need to go. I can only slump against her, clutch her other hand in mine as we twine together. Only later, much later, after she's wrung every last drop of pleasure out of me, can I return to what I've started with her. She's granted me a glimpse into another side of her, one I had previously only hoped existed, and it's hard to tell whether going there, to that land of my dreams, entering her so closely, will ultimately be the wisest choice, but it's the only one I can make in the moment. And in that moment, when she looks up at me so wide-eyed and full of wonder, it's worth anything it may later cost me, even if there's no going back.

Eventually, in the wee hours of the morning, she leaves, quietly, ducking her small frame through the door as she tiptoes out, thinking I won't notice. I don't know what to think, just watch her exit and feel my body convulse again in a combination of longing, arousal, and disappointment. She's still straight, and there's nothing easy about her, but I'm a total goner anyway.

EXERCISE
DYKE
CHERI CRYSTAL

I HAD JUST FINISHED my third set of bicep curls when I noticed this cute zaftig femme checking me out. At five-feet-six and 125 pounds of lean muscle mass, I was in peak physical condition for the triathlon coming up in June. All the rigorous training showed as my muscles rippled. I had no trouble lifting, running, swimming, or biking at top speed.

Since I wasn't the least bit tired, and she was obviously new around here, I decided to show off with another set, only with heavier weights. Wearing only a white A-line tank over a sports bra, I had free range of motion, but more importantly, the combo nicely accentuated my decent sized pecs and tight abs. The comfortable well-worn cutoffs were a tad too short, but I never minded the commotion they caused. I thought I would impress her with my powerful thighs while I was at it and walked over to the leg press.

Once I'd adjusted the equipment for my height, I tacked on sixty pounds, and sat down with my back against the padded seat. I grasped the handles tightly, making my biceps bulge. Okay, so I was making a big production out of it but I loved the attention. Forty pounds was usually my limit, since I preferred less weight and more reps for endurance rather than bulk, but I had an audience. With my feet squarely placed on the platform, I stretched and flexed my quads in slow fluid movements for emphasis. She watched me while she rocked back and forth on the StairMaster. It was impossible not to notice how gracefully she shifted her weight from one foot to the other in time to the background music. Thinner women weren't as light on their feet nor could they make climbing stairs look like ballet the way she did. As I watched her voluptuous breasts, wide hips, and solid thighs move in a syncopated motion with a captivating rhythm, I thought Reuben couldn't do justice to her.

I was mesmerized as she managed to put her whole body into the workout. I caught her eye and winked. A charming shade of red began at her more than ample cleavage, crept up her neck, and completely covered her round face. The color complimented her short burgundy hair. She quickly turned her attention to the mute TV.

I continued my workout, stealing glances in her direction every so often. She returned the favor as she worked out on the rowing machine. I loved what the equipment was doing to her breasts. She had great tits and when she pushed them out like that, I had a hard time keeping count for my own workout.

Her T-shirt fit snuggly over her large breasts and rounded abdomen, and ended at her well-proportioned hips. I always preferred women with curves I could hold on to and supple flesh I could sink my teeth into. This blushing redhead with the dimples, bright blue eyes, and roguish grin piqued my interest from the get-go.

I was still considering going over and asking her if she needed a spot, as she meandered in my general direction. Before I could make my move, she decisively approached the bench press.

"You really know what you're doing," she said, coyly.

"I guess," I said, deciding to play it cool. Up close, I got a whiff of her intoxicating earthy scent of sandalwood, amber, and patchouli.

The lip-gloss on her moist thick lips caught the light and glistened as she spoke.

"You look amazing," she said.

This time it was my turn to blush. I could feel the heat rising into my cheeks when I murmured, "Thanks."

"Mind helping me get into that kind of shape? I could sure use some pointers." She took a long and not so subtle moment to appreciate my breasts. I couldn't help but grin.

I squared my shoulders and sucked in my already

tight gut, further accentuating my chest. "Sure, I'd be happy to help."

"Great!" She closed the space between me and the bench. "What should I do first?"

"Well, let's see...have you sufficiently warmed up yet?"

"I'm always warmed up."

I looked intently into dark eyes that were becoming more black than blue from her enlarged pupils. Flustered, she looked away and played with the thick herringbone chain with a diamond studded "S," around her neck.

"KC, that's K-C," I said, and extended my hand. She took it in hers and held it longer than necessary. "And you?"

"Everyone calls me Sunny."

"Hey, nice to meet you. Let's get started then."

I gave her eight-pound free weights to start. I took her through three sets of ten with each exercise working the different muscle groups. Feeling the heat, I held her elbow in place to keep it still while she pushed the weight toward the back wall. The innocent touch inexplicably excited me as she worked on her triceps. Trying to come up with an excuse to hold on to her hips, I got a brilliant idea. Leg raises. She was on all fours in no time and I was very helpful in keeping her hips from swaying. I stifled a sigh as my hands held on to her succulent flesh. There was so much to love.

The all female gym I frequented was notorious for having plenty of dykes to fuel my workout and get my heart pumping. Earlier in the evening, women of all shapes and sizes stretched out on crowded mats. The exercise equipment seldom had a vacancy and the women were all there for the same thing. To get fit or to get laid. Or both. Usually I enjoyed the view but tonight I only had eyes for my curvy lady. We lifted and did cardio for over an hour before I realized how sweaty we were. We did some calisthenics but she was breathing too heavily for my comfort level. It was okay in bed, but not during a workout. I decided it was time to cool down and stretch.

"You okay?" I asked. It wasn't like I would mind doing CPR on those lips or massaging her chest but that wasn't the kind of romance I was fantasizing about.

"Yeah, just a bit winded. I'm fine. Better than fine."

I handed her my water bottle and she took a long drink with what seemed like an endless thirst I hoped I could quench.

I shook my head to clear my thoughts. "I hope we didn't overdo it your first time with a new exercise routine."

"Nah, I am getting into the hot tub to ease my muscles before I swim a few laps. Why don't you come?"

"That's a great idea. I'd love to." It was getting late and the gym was emptying. Good thing it was open twenty-four hours a day so there was no rush.

The endorphins from the intense workout had me horny as hell and the only thing that would feel better was to have her tongue on my clit. I bit my lip to keep from moaning at the thought. Excitement about changing into swimsuits got the better of me. I prayed her locker was in eyeshot. When my wish came true, I wondered what the odds of her locker being right next to mine were, and thought, *Did she plan this?* Somehow, the idea pleased me to no end.

My heart rate quickened, everything got blurry, and my libido went into high alert when she seductively removed her T-shirt to reveal a white lace bra that was two sizes too small. Her large breasts flowed over the top and out the sides. I longed to relieve the pressure; the fabric looked like it was constricting the blood flow, but she beat me to it. The brassiere landed on the floor and I couldn't pull my eyes away from her breasts with their bright red nipples all puckered and begging for attention.

I took off my wife-beater and bra. She didn't even bother to pretend she wasn't checking me out. After unzipping my fly, I quickly removed my shorts, taking the briefs underneath with them. I saw her bite her lower lip as if contemplating her next move. That's when her sweatpants came off. Who would have guessed she would have on French knickers?

I moaned despite myself. Seeing all that luscious pink flesh and her soft dark curls under white sheer lace made my clit ache. A strong current shot through my pelvis, almost knocking me to my knees. Her breasts were more than two handfuls, her round tummy just cried to be kneaded, and those shapely thighs, well, they really did me in. I couldn't take my eyes off her and she appeared to enjoy the attention.

"May I?" I asked, indicating her knickers.

"Yes, I was hoping you would help me with this part of the workout too."

I put my hands at the top of the lace and pushed them down over her thighs and to her knees before I let gravity take over. The knickers quickly made it to her ankles and she kicked them aside.

"You're beautiful," I said, before I could stop the words from escaping.

"No, *you* are. I'm too fat, but you're perfect."

"You're not fat, you've got a shape, unlike the scrawny models out there that are all skin and bones, feh!" I meant it. All I knew at that moment was that I wanted to get lost in all her glory.

As she rummaged around her bag for her bathing suit, I got a magnificent view of her butt. Suddenly I was getting very wet. I distracted myself by throwing all my clothes into the locker and slamming the door before everything tumbled out. The last thing I wanted to do was to put on a suit. I liked the birthday suits we both had on at the moment. She repeated her question, "How can I lose this weight? I am really following my diet but the scale won't budge lately."

"It's just a plateau. Listen, you really don't need to lose any weight, honestly. But, if you want to, then you should exercise at least three to four times a week, preferably more like six, vary your routine, and you'll get your metabolism up." With a cocky grin, I straightened my back and leaned in a bit closer. "Sex also helps curb the appetite for food and is a great way to burn calories," I added.

"I like that advice." She gave me her most mischievous smile, which extended all the way to her ears. "Want to help me shed a few pounds?"

A couple of dykes walked into the locker room. As soon as they saw us, they gave me a knowing look and hightailed it out of there. I was grateful for a little butch solidarity when warranted. I would do the same for them. Now the only sounds were the clock on the wall, the drip from a nearby sink, and the beat of my heart. I closed the space between us.

"Why don't we burn a few more calories right now then?" I leaned in to kiss her lips, which parted in anticipation of what was to come.

"Ummm, that sounds soooo good," she purred, and devoured my mouth with her thick lips and eager tongue.

I feasted on her slightly salty neck, taking little bites along the way. Her skin was soft and supple. The earthy scent of musk drowned out the smell of chlorine. I put my arms around her shoulders to steady myself, then laced my fingers in her stylish short-cropped hair and pulled her in even closer. Our breasts danced against each other as our tongues intertwined. Her large breasts enveloped my much less endowed ones, making me crazy with desire.

I covered her round butt with my hands and worked my way around the front, again biting and sucking in the ample flesh of her abdomen down to her soft damp curls. She used her nails to prickle my skin, sending goose bumps up and down my body. The pebbled flesh of my darkened nipples gave away how turned on I was but not as much as the pool forming between my thighs.

"How about that hot tub?" she suggested.

I took her hand and led her to the tub.

I set the timer on the jets to the max and we got in. I was on fire. The bubbles, like Champagne on an empty stomach, made me giddy. Although they obliterated my view of her naked body, I had no trouble locating her breasts for a quick squeeze, meanwhile nestling my thigh between her parted legs. I pulled her toward me for a kiss that left us both gasping for air. My hands were in her hair, over her back, and then down to her hips as I fiercely pulled her to me—I was getting close to climaxing but somehow I resisted the urge.

Sunny straddled my lap with her pussy as close to mine as possible.

"Geeze, Sunny," I murmured. She was killing me here and she looked quite pleased with herself. I had to distract myself or I would come and my rule was the lady always comes first.

I turned her buoyant body and positioned her clit not too close, but in direct line, of a jet stream. My fingers made their way into her crevices while the jet worked her clit. Her delight stirred me. Inspired by her music, I put my finger into her juicy cunt. She threw her head back over my shoulder and I kissed her cheek.

As a tease, I pulled her away from the jet and didn't give in when she started to protest. When we both couldn't take it anymore, I circled her engorged clit with my thumb. Her hips jerked as I increased the speed of my ministrations, thrusting my fingers in and out. Alternating between the jet and my thumb, I wanted to be sure that I made her come and not the water.

"Oh, K, ahhhh, yeah...God, just like that," she managed to speak as I fingered her clit slowly while finger fucking her at the same time. I angled her farther away from the stream of water but I never lost touch. The water aimed at my crotch was enough to send me over but I had work to do. I longed to taste her. Swiftly, I lifted her up and out of the water with the brute force of a warrior in heat. Her bare ass was on the side of the pool; I parted her legs and luscious folds as she carefully leaned back on her elbows. I devoured the feast in record time as the jets pummeled my breasts with wild abandon. It was a good thing I was flexible so I could spread my legs almost into a complete split. I felt like a circus performer juggling my clit in the jet and my tongue on her G-spot. Free to explore with my hands, I didn't know where to touch first. I loved it!

"K...C....I'm going to come. Don't stop. Don't–"

"Let it go, Sun. It's just the first of many." I didn't stop until her last wave ceased. I was nearing my own crescendo as the jet continued to massage my clit. Unable to prolong the torture, I gave in to pleasure and shook with each hot tub shattering spasm.

Climbing out of the tub, I was beside her in an instant. She looked lovely lying contentedly on her back. It was a flattering position, especially with me on top, I thought, feeling so full of myself. I cradled her head with my hand to protect her from the hard floor. Sunny looked up at me with lust still evident in her eyes.

I bestowed gentle kisses on her head, cheeks, and neck. I then took a nipple between my teeth and just as I bit down softly, she bucked and shuddered again. I felt like a king and as my loyal subject, she would do exactly as I pleased. It pleased me to give her pleasure. I never wanted to stop.

"I could really get into this type of exercise routine," she said and smiled.

"Like I said, six times a week should do it, but seven is even better." I winked.

"Sounds like a plan."

SHARP CLAWS, SOFT PAWS

EVA VANDETUIN

I WAS A NEW TOP, then. I'd beaten some girls, left satisfying stripes on a few, brought more than one to a screaming climax with alternating pleasure and pain. I adore pain—when other people are feeling it. And so does she: Andrea, Andi, Drea, Drei. Andrea at work; Andi to her parents and childhood friends; Drea to her college buddies; Drei in the scene. I like calling her by that last name best, the pert, androgynous monosyllable in contrast to the lush curves of her wide-spaced breasts, her full lips, the tangle of dark corkscrew curls that spiral merrily down her back. "Drei" is the name I whisper to her when she's about to come, and her already large dark eyes seem to expand impossibly to take up her entire face, her pupils black and wide and bottomless with desire.

It was during an orientation at the local sex-positive community center that I saw her first. The place was a kind of a cooperative version of a sex club, with a penchant for education and the occasional night of fully clothed canasta, and I was curious and looking for something a little less sleazy than the sex clubs I'd visited before. When I found myself feigning an air of mildly disinterested cool, I knew she'd caught my eye. I watched her as our tour guide bubbled on about the group's history, its auspicious birth in a convenient basement, and eventually flowering into the clean and well-maintained space where we sat in standard-issue folding chairs. She was listening more attentively than I was and occasionally making notes on her handout, her lips pursed. She pushed a stray curl back behind her ear, and I felt suddenly too aware of myself—slouched in my chair, suit coat slightly rumpled, boots a little scuffed. I'd wanted to be casual, my first visit to the center, but now I regretted not putting in a little more effort. Would a girl like that fancy a dyke who dresses like a forty-year-old man? And a slightly absent minded one at that.

We took the tour: the dance floor, the showers, the library, a hot wax room, a sex room filled with beds and clean linen, a BDSM room with racks and spanking benches. I was watching her when she saw the massive wooden bunk bed, fitted with strong metal eyebolts at dozens of points on the frame. "You can suspend up to three hundred pounds from this bed!" our guide enthused, and because I was watching her, I saw the look that flashed across her face: a kind of feral grin that lit her eyes with a flicker of submerged ferocity before it was gone, leaving her face again serene and attentive. I know a kindred spirit when I see one. Later, when the tour was done, I saw her fish a glass bottle of soda out of the snack bar fridge. In an instant I was at her side, offering the bottle opener off my keychain. It's a far goofier ploy than offering a light, but I did it with a ironic smile and looked her in the eye. After a moment, she smiled back, dazzling me with a flash of her sharp white teeth.

We chatted as the space slowly turned into a dance club around us and when the music started and people began to gather, I pulled her onto the dance floor. She moved confidently, her hips rolling independently of her rib cage like a belly dancer's; her eyes closed as her body caught the beat, then opened to meet mine. I saw her pelvis twitch toward me and felt a tingle in the pit of my stomach. *Ohhh, she does like me. Yes.*

An hour later found us wrapped around each other on a bed in the back room, mouths melded harmoniously as her fingers ruffled my hair and mine slid just under the hem of her shirt. Even that first night, she fit against me as if we were old lovers: her round breast nestled between my smaller ones, her cunt wedged comfortably between my hip and thigh. And maybe more would have happened that night if we hadn't been so eager to show our true colors, because we were kindred spirits in more ways than one. I dragged my nails down her back, too hard, and she stopped me with a wince; she pinched my nipple with too firm a grip and I ungracefully responded with "Ouch!" We backed off for a moment, considering, then resumed kissing, and left the club with each other's contact information in our pockets.

And so, on our first official date, we went to dinner and a movie, then stood in an alleyway and necked like teenagers. She squeezed my ass like she wanted to slap it, and I stroked her hair like I wanted to pull it, and when it was well past midnight we parted with knowing smiles, wondering if and when our beloved bags of toys were going to see the light of day and the soft glow of waiting, naked flesh. I wanted her, but remembering her smile I couldn't let go of the desire to give our play the special edge only pain could add.

Over the next few weeks when I touched myself I could think only of her. The sway of her walk, the delicate silver rings on her slim fingers... the sprinkling of soft, dark fuzz trailing down her spine from her hairline, and me closing my teeth on the nape of her... No. I dip my fingers into my cunt and flick my clit, letting go of the fantasy, trying another. She's on her stomach on my bed, her short black dress hitched up past her hips, a silk garter belt holding up smooth black stockings, her panties already crumpled on the floor. I'm pressing my favorite, thick red cock against her waiting cunt, pinning her wrists to the bed as I... No, no. A sweat breaks out on my forehead as my pelvis quivers beneath my increasingly desperate fingers. She's stripped bare in one of my wooden kitchen chairs and I'm kneeling in front of her, nibbling at her hot folds as her clit swells and begins to peek through, and she reaches down and...pulls my hair hard... Oh no. I pinch my nipple and think of her face and her eyes, the way her mouth feels on mine, and my body bucks with the orgasm in a spasm of unsatisfied agony. Immediately I want another climax, but instead I sit up and bite my knuckles, the tense racing of my mind in contrast to the pleasant post-orgasmic relaxation that I won't quite let take hold. Drei, Drei, oh Drei, I want to touch you, I want to connect with you, I want to hurt you, but I want you to like it...

And so we found ourselves at a stalemate, kissing, groping, looking for a way to give our first time together the intensity we both craved. When we couldn't be together, we were e-mailing and sending each other instant messages, leaving me in a state of perpetually aroused mania at work. I think my fellow techs thought I was on some hot new stimulant; when one asked me where he could get some of what I had, I smiled and said nothing.

A few weeks later an on-again, off-again lover of mine sent out invitations for a women-only play party at the large house she shared with roommates, and I jumped at the chance to invite Drei. That night I primped in a way I'd failed to the night we met: tomboy haircut carefully trimmed, leather pants freshly oiled, a shirt that fit tightly to my body and showed off my shoulders. I took out my piercings and shined them nervously.

When we arrived the party was already in full swing, with women in various states of undress lounging about the room, stuffing their faces with snacks, giving massages, gossiping. I peeked through one doorway to see an elaborate fisting session going on, one woman cradled in a pile of her friends and lovers while another delicately but uncompromisingly pushed in her hand deeper and deeper. In another room, two women worked on each other amongst a small arsenal of floggers, paddles, crops, canes, and other toys, evaluating each with a critical eye before trying it experimentally on buttocks and thighs. Drei joined me to watch, eyes shining, her gaze dwelling affectionately on one particularly soft and lovely flogger, the tails sprawled languidly on the floor.

Abruptly I felt enthusiastic arms wrap around my neck and a pair of soft lips on my cheek. "Lou, honey, I'm so happy you could make it!" I heard Gina squeal, and I turned to hug her back and lift her off her feet—her small, lithe body completely naked, as usual when she wasn't in public. "Oh, and you must be Drei! I've been looking forward to meeting you," Gina added, kissing Drei on the cheek as well. Drei's eyes widened in pleased surprise, and I saw her watch Gina appreciatively as the slightly built young woman turned back to me, her blue eyes bright. I could tell Drei was staring at her ass, because Gina had a delightfully round one, with skin that marked beautifully on impact but rapidly faded.

I played with Gina's hair lovingly, tugging on the soft shocks of red. "I bet girls are lining up to beat you tonight, sweetheart, but I'd love to be on your list."

Gina gave a girlish laugh. "You're in luck, actually. I'm totally free at the moment. I even have a couple of new toys you can try out."

I threw Drei a glance as an idea started to form in my head. "Mind if I assist?" she asked politely, and Gina readily agreed.

We settled in one of the bedrooms to unpack, and I found myself growing warm with anticipation at the impressive collection of toys that we arrayed around us, ready and waiting. A few partygoers stuck their heads in to admire the proceedings; one offered a heavy rubber paddle that we added to the mix. Drei's favorite flogger and mine lay nestled together like old friends: hers, soft and black with red braided into the handle, mine a bit heavier, with red tails and a handle braided with black, the two together like a hers-and-hers set. I paused a moment, resting my fingertips on my flogger handle like a greeting, remembering the feel of it in my hand, the sound of it striking flesh. Almost, I thought I saw its tails quiver in anticipation.

And then we began. We started lightly, with rabbit fur and then a tiny, stingy light flogger, moving up slowly to heavier leather ones, adding canes and paddles, moving rhythmically over Gina's prone body. Soon her face relaxed into a blissful smile, her eyes opening occasionally as she asked for this toy used a little harder, that one a little more lightly. We marked her like artists working on a pristine white canvas, an angry splotch of red here, a half-circle of pink highlighting the curve of her buttock, even stripes of blush and white decorating her shoulders. I kept my eyes on Gina, but I was equally aware of Drei as we moved together in a dance of bodies and flying tails, the slap and thud of wood and rubber and leather on flesh providing the beat. Gina's skin bloomed rosily under our ministrations as we worked, switching toys from hand to hand as we circled her slowly, and when Drei handed off a flogger to me and I brought it down on Gina's buttock without breaking rhythm, I didn't notice the exchange's uncanny smoothness until minutes later.

We brought Gina down gently with softer and softer toys, finishing with the rabbit fur flogger and firm, kneading strokes of our hands, loosening the muscles beneath her flushed skin even further. When she finally raised her head I knew it had gone well. "That was beautiful, y'all," she said dreamily, giving us each a tender kiss. Gina's tongue was wet in my mouth and I blushed to feel Drei watching, sensing rather than seeing her slow grin. Drei and I sat on either side of Gina, stroking her hair, and Drei's pupils were large, her color high from the mild exertion. She looked at me, and as our fingers met on Gina's back, I felt a sizzle between us like a shock from a car door on a dry winter day. "You two are well-matched," Gina murmured, and when Drei smiled her tight, fierce smile, I knew tonight would be the one.

We stumbled together into a temporarily empty bedroom, clawing at each other's clothes until they dropped away from us like discarded skins, and fell onto the bed already kissing, still flushed and warm from the thrill of giving pleasure and pain. Drei's hands stroked gently down my back as I touched her, feeling her wet and open under my fingers. Mouths pulled delicately at nipples, tongues searched out erect clits, and soon we were both breathing hard as we pressed slick bodies together, lips close but not touching, breathing hot gasps into each other's mouths. There was an ache in my belly, yearning toward her, and then I saw the flash of her teeth in the dim light before she bent to whisper in my ear. "Now. I want to fuck you. Now." She wouldn't let me pleasure her without also pleasuring myself, so I reached for the thick black double-ended from my toy bag. I'd only just eased the egg-shaped "active" end into myself, intending to take her on her back, when she pushed me forcibly down on mine and positioned herself over the aggressive black phallus that jutted from my cunt. "I want you," she said, and shoved herself down over me, her eyes rolling up into her head as she reached for my nipples and caressed them—gently, attentively. I massaged her clit with eager fingers, and before long the climaxes began, each of us rolling continuously from one peak to the next as we fucked each other deeply. For a while, I forgot everything but her, everything but the feeling of flesh melting into flesh, our hips grinding together in such perfect rhythm that we seemed like one body rather than two. She looked epic mounting me this way, like a warrior queen out of a Greek myth, her back arching, her hands tightening in her own hair as a new bout of ecstasy seized her. Drei stared down me as if she would devour me, and I imagined sinking my teeth into her shoulder, but instead we only touched each other softly, the desire to slap and scratch and bruise already satiated.

At the end of the night we stumbled out in each other's arms, kissing Gina again in delight and gratitude, not caring about the silly grins plastered across our faces. My sadist lover and I are going home to make pancakes and cuddle in the blankets and stare dreamily into each other's eyes—for we have begun to see each other now, all the beloved parts that have teeth and claws and a fierce, bloody hunger. But she does not have to sink her claws into me for me to know her.

I think I will have to send Gina flowers, tomorrow....

THE STOCK CONTRACTOR'S
DAUGHTER
RAKELLE VALENCIA

I RIDE BULLS. I'M not talking about strictly chasing the rodeo circuit. I'll cinch myself onto snorting, snot-blowing, frothy sons-of-pot-roast any time, anywhere. It's a disease. It's gotten into my blood.

I need rodeo. I need the bulls. Just the thought of the ride and I can smell it, taste it, and feel my skin get clammy in the hot sun. The thought alone entices me to run my tongue over dried lips, imagining grinding the grit from between my teeth and scratching at my dust-covered face with a rosin-sticky gloved hand grasping a limp bull rope. The thought can bring these sensations back vividly, so much so that I can't help but yearn for the next ride. It's powerful. And, it makes me horny.

I need to strap myself onto that power. Adrenaline courses from my head and my toes to pool in my groin. I need that feeling of being on something so out of control, so bestial, that it takes me with it and all I can do is hold on, humping and writhing and bucking.

A wild, thrashing rhythm surges between my legs. I'm compelled to stay on top of it for what seems an eternity of intensity, building but giving no release.

There's no sense in the sport. Those bulls aren't ever going to stop hopping. And each time there is only one way off. Yah, gettin' off is gonna hurt, whether I made the buzzer or not, whether I made the ride or not.

The bulls offer no internal release. The ride leaves me pent up. When I've taken my pounding and am climbing out of the sand, stumbling in a frenzied run for safety while that big, spotted bull blows hot air at the back of my britches, smearing my batwings chaps with green snot and saliva, I know I haven't had enough. I need something more.

Six seconds to meet the buzzer at the gay rodeo competitions isn't nearly enough for me, even if I am lucky to make the ride. It only winds me up. I feel my balls swell to gigantic proportions. But of course I don't really have any. I walk taller, strut, hitch at my leather chaps and shove my cowboy hat off my forehead for the appearance of serenity. Truth is, I'm ready to pop.

What I really want to do is grab my crotch, and run a hand into my tight, Jockey boxer briefs smearing at the growing wetness to jerk off quick and rough. Of course I can't do that, not right here, not at the busy chutes of the arena. But I want to. I want to rub up against something, anything, because in my head my ride isn't over, my ride has just begun.

Even more torturous, the "buckle polishers" rush from the grandstands after the events have quieted and the winners are projected. They press their supple bodies to me in congratulations, sliding their hips against my own, earning their title for putting the shine on my waistline hubcap. And any one of them would do.

I want one. I want to fill my hands with their ass cheeks and grind them to me, throwing my head back as it would snap while on a bucking bull. And I feel urgency greater than the need to mount angry hamburger.

Like that weekend rodeo back in August when I was observing the scene of buckle-polishers corralled behind the grandstand fences as I bent over to tuck my rope and glove into a dust-covered gear bag. I had convinced myself that one of them would do. One of them *had* to do.

I judged them like the bulls, looking over their length, and what they brought to the ride. I couldn't see their eyes, but I could tell in their movement what they had. I knew first if it would have been worth the go around, and second if I could have stayed with them to the buzzer. If it wasn't gonna be worth the ride, I wouldn't cinch my rope down onto one. I wasn't playing at any high school rodeo finals. That weekend was the Atlantic Stampede of the International Gay Rodeo Association, for crying out loud.

My choice from the two-legged stock had been basically all femmes in their wanna-be country outfits. There was a petite chick in a straw hat three-sizes too big with a plastic flower peeking over the edge. She had worn white, unblemished, pointy-toed, cockroach killers, with fringe flopping in a line down the sides of those boots. Well, I'd have given her a good ride. I could tell she was sweet, and I could have almost tasted her on my tongue. But she wasn't what I had needed that weekend. I had needed something more sporting.

With a gear bag jerked over my shoulder, I exited the arena through the grandstand area. Why shouldn't I have? Since they were advertising, I wasn't gonna sneak out the back door.

The wave parted and hands had stroked the length of my ripped arms as I traveled through. And there *she* was, my evening's ride. Not forward in the least, but not hanging back. She was waiting, thinking. At that point I had gotten close enough to her to see the look in her eyes. There was a gleam in those baby-blues, calculating, sizing *me* up. And I should have known then that there was something more about her. But as the saying goes, I was thinkin' with the little head.

She had stood out in one way, the way you could blend into reality. The woman was authentic. With a serious work shirt, Sunday-go-to-meeting, newer Wranglers, and clay-encrusted Roper boots to match, scratched by the attempt of small bristles to clean them, probably a horse-grooming, rice-root brush, this woman was a cowboy. And she was no lady, the emphasis being on *boy* in cowboy.

"You got a pickup truck?" I asked. She nodded. "The bed open?"

"Yup."

She had tipped her hat at the handful of still milling women as we exited. The move made me wonder if I had a dandy on my hands; you know, all show and no go. I shifted the weight on my shoulder. *Was the pathetic Chevy S-10 alone in the parking lot hers?*

"Around here," she had said, flipping her hat-covered head to the side of the arena, a considerable hike away.

"What? Did you get the cheap seats?" No answer, so I had followed silently, still toting my weighty gear.

"That's my truck." She pointed to a shined, chromed rig to make a pappa proud. "You could put your gear in there, but you might want to bring it inside." The cowboy reached to unlatch a camper trailer door.

"Riley and Sons?" *The stock contractors.* I knew my eyebrows had risen involuntarily in mild surprise, but I dropped one brown brow instantly, changing over to a look of consternation. *The stock contractor's daughter.*

"Dad's alright. Always wanted strapping boys. He got them. Me and three brothers. Four good, strong boys."

I had clicked the door behind me with a shit-eating grin and dropped my bag to the carpeted floor. I had the stock contractor's daughter. Better than that, I had a boi.

"Beer?" The boi had asked, shucking his wide brim hat to expose a sleek crew-cut, with a cowlick over his left eye standing in a half-moon arc, unmashed by his smudged, felt Stetson.

I shook my head. "Huh-uh," I muttered while my hand slipped absentmindedly to stroke the crotch of my jeans. If I had been hot to go that short while previous, I wasn't thinking I'd be able to hold back right then.

"I see," he had said. "I can help take care of that."

He shed his clothes in a no nonsense way, like a dog shaking off water, not hurried but fast. He had a small patch of trimmed pussy hair, barely noticeable as more than stubble. His body was hard just like mine, only stockier, thicker around the mid-section where my own waist narrowed to twenty-eight lean inches.

We were too much alike and then some. I wasn't a boi, but I could play at one. I was often mistaken for one, which had always been fine by me. It left me wondering though if we were going to have to flip a coin or flip each other. I thought that maybe I had the wrong ride. I did have needs that night, desperate needs that had to be met right then and there, so I was in for the long haul.

Cocking my head to the side and pondering my predicament, I had slowly pulled tired, tight muscles out of cotton, dust-caked clothes, watching, waiting. Not in too much of a hurry now, guessing that I had probably chosen the wrong date. And in my mind the femme with those "cockroach killers" and the floppy hat had sadly been looking better and better in Daisy Dukes.

The boi sauntered over to help, surprising me by thrusting experienced fingers into my twat and hitting all of the right spots immediately. I hadn't considered myself easy, but he took me in three. I jerked and jumped almost going to my knees.

Hot breaths of air tickled my ear as he moved in, pressing his own body to hold me up. "Are you here to ride?" he had asked low, almost hoarse, vibrating my inner ear, driving my core to shiver.

"Yah," I grunted between clenched teeth as another wave of spasms took control.

"Let's do it," he said with a slight sneer, backing away, licking at each of his creamed fingers. He turned toward the kitchen cabinetry to pull at drawers.

He had a lovely ass, high and tight, not too bulbous. I had to have a piece of that—which prompted me to reach into my gear bag and yank out a tangled harness. As I was shaking the straps loose, kicking off my boots and peeling my long legs from slim fit Wranglers still half on, the boi had turned to wait with an assortment of cock dongs filling his tanned, working hands.

"One size does not fit all. And I don't bareback." He flipped several different condoms at me with hidden dexterity, then examined and contemplated his dicks.

Purple, he had chosen the purple silicone dong that had to have been over six inches, and rippled down the rubbery length. Tossing it to me, he reached for a tub of half-gone waxy lube. He smeared his crack with copious amounts, filling it to oozing.

Then the boi dropped to his knees and went down on the dong that nestled in my nylon harness, tucked securely against me so as to stick straight out vying for attention.

His sweet mouth worked the prick with such talent that I truly believed he was worshipping a part of me.

The boi made me feel as if that dick was alive. He made me ache to enter him. He made me need to fuck his little brown, puckered hole. And the boi knew this.

He dragged me by the dick to a sleeping alcove, bent over and braced himself, flagging that tight, white ass at me. The waxy cream glistened as if to point the way to his slippery hole. It wasn't the type of riding that I had envisioned doing that evening, but I wasn't complaining now.

Sheathing in a lubricated condom, I slicked the prick up and down his crack, hooking his hole, stopping a moment to teasingly probe its give. He was ready. I've never seen an asshole more ready. The puckered entrance almost sucked my dick into its cavity like a Hoover vacuum.

"Fuck me. No girlie warm-ups. Fuck me," he said.

With that, I did. I had pounded his ass, sinking home to a slapping sound with each thrust. He moaned and groaned causing my rhythm to pump faster. "You fuck like a girl," he hissed through clenched teeth.

I knew I didn't. I was all about the ride, the rhythm, the ever-increasing intensity until an explosion ripped loose. I knew I didn't fuck like a girl. A bull rider doesn't fuck like a girl. He was taunting me. And it worked.

My roughened, calloused hand reached around to cover his trimmed pussy, stroking and plucking the hardened nodule hidden within its crease. His groans gave way to screams and obscenities. My dong was caught in a human vice, stopping my action, and toppling us into the bed, bruising my shin on the wooden ridge of the camper's padded structure.

Our sweaty bodies slipped and rolled onto cool cotton sheets, disengaging my prick with a soft sucking sound. I released the clasp on the nylon harness and kicked the ensemble to my ankles.

The dick had fallen to the sawdust-strewn carpet, but there were other dicks. I reached for the one with a curved tip and straddled the downed boi, much like towering over a captured bull in the chute. I carefully draped my harness rigging, and rolled the boi. Cinching and buckling the straps into place, my ride was ready. All I had to do was lower myself onto it, nod to the gate, and come crashing and thrashing from the chutes.

Instead of the rosin-stick, I wanted it slick. My hungry cunt had obliged by welling another load of cream between my legs, and dribbling my thighs. Dumping onto the beast, onto my human ride, I expected immediate action.

The dong reached into me. The curved end seared my G-spot, prodding as it slid. I jumped and rode hard in little humping movements. But I had seemingly rode alone.

The boi's eyes were half-lidded, heavy with sleep. He lay there in languor, succumbing to an after-orgasm coma. *Wasn't he the one to have chastised my vigor? Wasn't he the one to have baited me into fucking like a runaway jackhammer?*

Reaching between his legs, I goaded by pumping at his clit. He bucked a bit with my effort, like me taking spurs to a bull in a spin, digging the inside and rolling the outside to get a better performance. Hell, I had been there for the ride. It was the ride I wanted and needed, and I damned well better get.

I jabbed at him again, losing my middle finger into the wasted heat of him. Then he came alive. We went humping and dumping all over the bed alcove. He bucked so hard it had thrown the top of my skull into the upper bunk board with a monstrous thunk.

The camper rocked and I didn't know what had squeaked, the straining floorboards or the dry axles. The ride went wild. I hung on because that was what I liked, what I needed, out of control power taking me completely with it.

The boi had a gleam in his blue eyes, a fire that I hadn't suspected. He knew that. He knew all of it, and he balls-sure knew what I needed out of my rides, out of my life. And he had given it all to me in that one night.

I had been a cocky bull rider, sizing up stock. He had been the stock contractor's daughter, sizing up cocky bull riders.

FINDING PERSPECTIVE

ANDREA DALE

IS THERE ANYTHING SO depressing as being away from your lover on Valentine's Day?

It doesn't matter that Cheryl and I have had reservations at a beachfront hotel in Cambria for almost a year. When my boss says go, I pretty much have to go.

So here it is, February fourteenth in Burlingame (because, of course, any decent hotel in San Francisco has also been booked for months, if not years). I ordered a take-out pizza earlier, not wanting to watch the cute couples in a restaurant while I sat alone. The box is still open on the other bed. The smell of hour-old, oregano-laced tomato sauce isn't appealing anymore, but it's too cold outside to open a window.

If Cheryl were here, we'd open the window, and then create some serious friction before snuggling under the covers.

God, I sound so maudlin. It's just a day, right?

Cheryl thought about coming with me but she ended up being on call—the midnight shift—at the vet clinic.

She called me at lunchtime, and text-messaged me about two hours ago, a bunch of exxes and ohs.

We disgust people with our mutual cuteness sometimes, and do so with great pleasure.

I'm lying on the bed, still full from the pizza, flipping channels. There's nothing on, of course, except *When Harry Met Sally*, *Everybody Loves Raymond* (except me), and basketball. And CNN. Like anyone wants to watch CNN on Valentine's Day.

I'm actually desperate enough to think about grabbing the laptop and doing some work. Thank goodness my cell phone rings and saves me. I tuck the bud in my ear and answer.

"Hello, Kitten," Cheryl says.

She calls me that because the first time we had sex, I scratched her back when I came (it really was that good). Sometimes all I have to do to get her hot now is to flex my imaginary claws.

"Thank god," I say. "You've saved me from another maudlin Rachel/Ross *Friends* rerun."

She laughs. She has this delighted laugh that infects you with little bubbles of joy. Her nose wrinkles when she laughs, and I just want to sprinkle kisses on it, and all over her face, and then all over her body, until laughter isn't the noise she's making anymore.

She makes some really nice noises. Breathy little moans that turn into pleasure-filled screams.

I glance at the clock. She should be leaving for work in about ten minutes.

"I missed you," she confesses, her voice husky. "Actually, I'm missing you a lot."

Something about the way she says it makes me tingle. "How much?"

"Enough to make me risk being late to work. I can't stop thinking about you, all alone in that hotel room, and what we'd be doing if I were there with you."

My heart makes a hard, almost painful thump against my breastbone. Isn't it silly, even when you've been with someone for a while, that the smallest change can feel so big? Just being away from her, in an unfamiliar place, and hearing her voice on the phone, makes me a little shy, and at the same time, a little bold.

I'm not the most articulate in bed at the best of times—I just get too distracted—and being far away from her makes her seem distant. But I'm lying here, clutching the phone in my sweaty hand, and I want her to tell me how much she's missing me, in minute, excruciating detail.

And I want to return the favor.

"Well, you're in luck," I say. "I'm not wearing much more than I would be if you were here."

Her breath catches. "Tell me."

"Dark green panties and your Beck T-shirt."

"I was wondering where that had gotten to."

"It smelled like you." Yeah, I'm enough of a sap to snag my lover's T-shirt out of the laundry bin before I leave on a trip.

"It looks a lot better on you than it does on me," she says. "It just molds to your gorgeous breasts."

Which is a nice way of saying that she's more petite than I am, but the fact is, she's right. The T-shirt hugs my curves, and my nipples are plainly visible, pressing against the soft, many-times-washed cotton.

I tell her that, how my nipples are hard already.

"You're getting ahead of me," she says. "You're so easy. It turns me on how quickly you respond."

"When given the right incentive," I say, meaning her. Which she knows.

"Tell me about the room," she asks. "I want to imagine you in it."

I describe the fairly generic, mid-range room: two beds (one for sex and one for sleep, we always joke), prints of pastoral scenes on the wall, a desk and chair and data port, a sturdy media armoire in nondescript blond wood.

"I'm on the left-hand bed. I've kicked the bedspread onto the floor and the blanket's all scrunched down. Oh, and I stole all the pillows off the other bed."

She's laughing again, probably because I'm so predictable.

"I had my hair up for the site visit today, but I took it down when I changed out of my suit," I add to her visuals.

"Mmm, I love how your hair smells."

"And I love to trail it all over your naked body," I say, almost surprising myself. It's true, though. I'll flip my hair over my head and run it along her breasts, her belly, making her squirm. I love the look of the dark brunette of my hair against the paleness of her skin. She's a cross between a redhead and a blonde—ash blonde on her head, but a color nearing ginger between her thighs.

"It feels so good when you do that," she agreed. "Like silk. My skin gets hypersensitive and it's like I can feel your hair touching me everywhere."

"I wish you were here touching me everywhere," I say, feeling wistful.

"Pretend that I am," she says. Her voice has changed again, from playful to sexy. "Play with your nipples like I would. No, over the shirt," she adds, as if she can see that I was reaching for the hem to pull it up. She knows me that well, I guess.

Thank goodness for the phone ear bud, leaving my hands free. I cup my breasts in my hands, then slide my hands up over the curves to run my palms over my peaked nipples. So sensitive, so ready, just from talking to her. I suppose she might want to tease me, but it's just me and I don't want to wait. I whimper.

"Tell me," she whispers.

I describe how I'm pinching my nipples, rolling them between thumb and forefinger. A little hard, just on the edge of pain. Rough play on my nipples makes me so wet so fast. I'm lightly scraping my nails over the hard points, my hips moving restlessly on the bed as the sensations streak down between my legs.

"Pull up your shirt now. Keep using your nails."

I'm moaning into the phone, twisting my nipples, catching them between my nails and rhythmically squeezing. I think I'm coherent enough to say something about how maybe we should try playing with light nipple clamps sometime, and I hear her indrawn breath again.

"Tell me what you're doing," I beg, but she just tells me how hot I'm making her, and then, "Are your panties wet? Reach down and touch them, lightly, on the outside, and then tell me."

Are my panties wet? Does the world turn?

I bend my knees and run my fingers between my thighs.

"God, yes, I'm wet. I've soaked my panties through. I can smell myself."

"Hot and sweet," she says. "You taste so good. Slip your hand inside your panties and get your fingers wet, then taste yourself. Taste what I taste when I'm licking you."

It takes all of my self-control to not just bring myself off right there and then. I barely flutter across my clit, because any greater pressure and I'll shoot off like a rocket. I part my lips and dip my middle finger into my cunt. Slick, hot. I bring my hand to my mouth, and tell her.

"It's good, isn't it?" she asks. "Don't ever wonder why I want to bury my face in you."

"Only if I get to return the favor."

"No complaints from me. Okay, Kitten, do something for me. Stroke yourself. Just play. I don't want you to come just yet." She's gasping a little, as if she's been exercising. Or playing with herself. I want to ask her, but I'm running out of words.

I've got to slow down a little, so I pull away and caress the insides of my thighs, the skin there hypersensitive. I use my other hand on my nipples again, alternating between them.

I tell Cheryl how I'm sprawled on the bed with my legs wantonly spread. She tells me to take off my panties, and I wriggle out of them. I touch myself again, spreading my nether lips and slipping two fingers inside. I feel myself flex around them, but I hold myself back from really coming. I spread my juices on either side of my clit, stroking nearby without touching full-on.

"I'm really close," I gasp. "I'm not sure how long I can hold off. Come with me."

"Wait," she says, a sharp command that surprises me a little. Reluctantly I pull my hands away. I could ignore her and turn off the phone mic and bring myself off, but I don't want the game to end just yet.

"Hurry and catch up," I say, assuming she wants me to hold off until she's almost ready, too.

"Do you know what I'm doing?"

"Masturbating, I hope!"

"Nope."

I hear the laughter bubbling in her voice again. My lust-fogged brain isn't comprehending this. "Why not?" I ask.

"Because I'm standing outside your hotel room door. You won't believe the looks I'm getting from other guests walking by. I think one of them is going to call security, so you'd better open up and let me in."

I scramble off the bed as fast as my trembling thighs let me, pulling the T-shirt back down. I didn't bother to bring a robe, so I snatch a towel from the bathroom and wrap it around my waist.

I peer through the peephole. All I can see is "267" on the door across from mine.

Please tell me she isn't joking.

I open the door.

She steps into my line of vision, her face split into a grin. She's holding a bottle of champagne and her cell phone and an overnight bag.

"But—but how—?"

She pushes me inside, drops the bag and the phone, and kisses me, really hard. Her tongue dances against mine, and I lose the concept of breathing. I can't get enough of the taste of her, the feel of her, and I'm hugging her so tight I'm afraid I'm going to hurt her.

She solves the problem by wriggling out of my grasp and plonking the champagne on the dresser.

"I managed to swap shifts with Dr. Boscoe," she says. "I wanted to surprise you." She reaches up and gently slips the bud out of my ear, turns off my phone, sets it next to the champagne. "I wanted to be with you on Valentine's Day."

My heart is pounding again, this time from the surprise, and I can't stop smiling. I want to pick her up and swing her around the room in a mad happy dance, but even more than that, I want to crawl back onto those hotel sheets and be responsible for her making those breathy noises and impassioned screams.

We get her clothes off in record time, strewing them all over the room. I lost the towel when I was kissing her, and she just pushes the T-shirt back up, and tells me to lie back on the bed like I was and play with my nipples again.

Her short hair tickles my inner thighs as she nuzzles up between my legs. She buries her tongue inside me, as deep as she can get it to go, and already my world is starting to shimmer and spin.

"So good," she moans, and I'd agree if I could form syllables beyond gasps and whimpers.

Then she's flicking her tongue against my throbbing clit and sliding fingers inside of me, and my fingers on her shoulders curl and once again, sobbing and bucking, I leave scratches on her smooth back.

When the room's whirling slows, I return the favor, sucking and nibbling and caressing her writhing body. She screams my name.

I'm thankful nobody calls the front office and complains.

Later—much later, after steamy sex and warm champagne and cold pizza—we open the window and snuggle under the covers, legs entwined. Cheryl's breathing evens and I start to drift off myself.

We don't need the hotel on the beach in Cambria. Oh, it would be nice—but we can do it any time we have a free weekend.

Everything I want for Valentine's Day I've got right here in my arms.

I AIM TO TEASE

YURI

AFTER ANOTHER RELATIONSHIP FAILED, I go to Buzz, the only lesbian bar in the city—alone. The cab drops me off in front of the door and I'm a little worried about seeing my ex here, but I can't stay in my apartment any longer. The smoke hits me as I enter and head directly for the bar, past the tables of dykes and their girlfriends. As I sit on the barstool, I have to pull down my miniskirt and cross my legs.

"What'll you have, sweetness?" the crew-cut bartender asks as she places a paper napkin in front of me.

"Something fruity," I say. The bartender turns away

from me. "With cherries in it please," I add. She nods her acknowledgement before fixing my drink.

"Tequila sunrise," the bartender says, handing me a pink glass with two cherries resting on top of the ice, stems still attached. I draw my wallet from my back pocket and hand her a five. In return, she hands me a few quarters. Suddenly, I remember why I hate coming to bars. Slightly disgusted, I take the change and toss it into the tip jar.

I offer her an unheard thank you before taking my drink onto the dance floor. It's after midnight and the women are on the prowl.

Bois and kings line the walls, too cool to let loose. While the jocks with their easy air and femmes, delighting in the attention, grind each other into a fever pitch. One of the tables opens up so I take a seat to watch the madness. Eventually, I will get out on the floor, but not yet. I need a few more drinks in me first. There's a wonderful freedom to be had when you release your body to the beat.

From my hidden place, I subconsciously scan the room for possibilities. I am, by no means, ready for a relationship—but everyone has needs. Connecting with a new woman never gets old. Sipping my drink, I let my mind wander from this girl to that, appreciating the different shapes and sizes of the immaculate female form. My eyes fall on a handsome boi on the other side of the room, staring in my direction, behind the glasses that reflect light so I can't see her eyes. The corners of her lips curl into a smile making me blush. Quickly, I avert my eyes and focus on the cherries in my glass.

I take the first one between my lips and chew the fruit, leaving the stem in my mouth. My tongue swirls it around until I firmly tie it into a knot. It started as a silly trick I thought would score me girls in college. Well, there were a few that found it fascinating, but for the most part it has become a habit of mine.

"Do you always drink alone?" a smooth alto voice says just beside me as I take the knotted stem from my mouth. I feel her words go though my ears, down my spine, and between my legs.

"No, not usually," I say just as smoothly. She doesn't need to know I had to take a cab here because I had a few glasses of wine before I came. Before I look at her, I re-cross my legs to release some of the heat. When I turn, I find the same beautiful brown-haired boi in her hockey jersey leaning against my table. I wave to the seat next to me but she doesn't sit. I swear, sometimes a jersey is the best aphrodisiac.

"Do you want another?" She points to my nearly full glass.

"Sure," I say before drinking the rest of the fiery liquid. To calm its protests as it burns my throat, I chase it with the other cherry. The beautiful boi takes my glass, leaving me tequila-warm, and she walks back to the bar. My eyes watch the easy swagger of her jeans until she's out of sight.

Femmes will always have a place in my heart, but there's something about a masculine woman that makes me blush.

I turn back to the dance floor. In the center of the mass of estrogen, surrounded by what looks like the first string of a WNBA basketball team, my ex shakes her hips to the bass. Our eyes meet briefly, but long enough for her to give me a drunken wave. I guess she also left that other girl? Maybe I should leave? I look to the door to see the jersey girl returning with a glass and beer in hand.

"Sorry, there was a crazy line at the bar," she says as she places my pink drink in front of me before sitting down. Resting atop the ice, five cherries sit. "I wanted to see what you would do with them."

"I'm Olivia," I say as I place the first juicy fruit across my lips.

"Ray," she says taking a drink of her beer.

"So, Ray, what brings you out tonight?" I ask still trying to maintain my cool.

"Just trying to get laid," she says as her arm drapes across the back of my chair. Even in my drunken state, her words shock me for a moment and I take a drink from my glass before I can speak.

"Well Ray, this may be your lucky night. Do you see that pretty blonde in the center of that basketball huddle?" I point to my ex who's become the cream filling of a six-footer sandwich.

"Yeah."

"Two weeks ago, I caught her in bed doing things we hadn't done for six months." I reach for my glass and take another drink. From the floor, I can feel my ex's eyes like a spotlight and sure enough, when I send a quick glance in her direction our eyes meet again. Let her watch me and realize what she lost. I swivel in my seat to brush the denim that covers Ray's legs. Then, I let my hand slide from my knee to hers briefly before bringing it atop the table.

"I want to see your eyes," I tell Ray as I bring my hand through her short brown hair and reach around the back of her ear to unhook the reflective glasses. She covers my drunken hand and together we remove them to reveal deep blue eyes.

"Why would you ever cover these up?" I ask breathlessly. Ray leans in allowing me to get lost in her eyes.

"Do you like them?" she asks as her arm leaves her chair and finds its way around my shoulders.

"Yes." My sandal slides along the inside leg of her jeans. "Do you want to get out of here?"

"Sure." Ray releases my shoulders to stand, then offers her hand to me. On wobbly legs, I rise and adjust my skirt. Ray's arm finds its way around my waist as we walk around the chaos on the dance floor and back toward the bar. I let myself lean against her, also wrapping an arm around her waist.

"Olivia!" A hand grabs my elbow, nearly forcing us around. "Are you leaving so soon?" My ex stands before me hot and sweaty from the dance floor. "I was hoping you would dance with me."

"It's too noisy tonight. See ya." I turn away from her and Ray and I leave the bar.

"That went smoothly," Ray says as we walk out of the bar

"What do you mean?" I ask. Ray's arm tightens around

me as we move to a very expensive looking car.

"You know how it is. Usually, two exes can't meet without someone throwing a punch," she says as she opens the door for me.

"I'm not that kind of girl." I laugh.

•

ALL THE WAY BACK to my apartment I keep my hand planted on Ray's denim-clad thigh. My fingers squeeze a steady rhythm up her thigh until I can feel the warmth radiating from between her legs and her hand covers my own drawing me away, keeping it closer to her knee. From there, I take my hand and begin brushing it though her short brown hair.

When we reach my apartment complex I wait for her to open the car door and I lead her by the hand to my apartment. I fumble with drunken fingers for my keys when Ray's soft lips begin nibbling the back of my neck. I can't concentrate on the keys and just rest my head against the door. She takes my hands, drawing them up on either side of us, palms flat against the door, while her hips press against mine forcing them against the door.

"Do you like this?" she says between bites. "Do you like being forced against the door?"

"We have to get inside," I gasp. Ray releases one of my hands and turns the key in the door lock. She pushes the door open, catching me around the waist so I don't fall with it, making me feel small and demure. After steadying myself, I walk in like a schoolgirl with my hands folded in front of me.

"Nice place," Ray says, closing the door behind her. She tosses my keys onto the couch.

"My bedroom is nicer," I say. Ray stands beside me and I wrap my arms around her waist, rising out of my sandals to kiss her face. The grin on her face tells me all I need to know as we lock hands and walk to my bedroom. I only release her hand when I reach my bed and spread out across the sheets, like a cat in heat. I move my hips slowly, so she can see them rock rhythmically from side to side. When I roll onto my back I find Ray standing at the end of my bed with her hands buried in her pockets.

I slide to the edge of the bed, letting my legs dangle between hers. My hands find the zipper of her jeans and slowly tug at the protruding metal nib. Again, she stops me and finishes unzipping her pants, letting them drop to the floor. She draws back her jersey revealing nine inches of firm latex with every curve of the real thing. She erects it within tongue's length from my mouth.

"It's new," she says. "You'll be the first."

"Um," I moan as I nip the tip of it with my teeth all the while gauging the reaction on her face. Then I flick it with my tongue, gaining a gasp from Ray. Her hands tangle in my hair as I ease her dick into my mouth. My head begins to bob back and forth and I wish she could really feel what I'm doing. I want to reach the woman behind the phallus, so I let my hands slide around her thighs. When I get close, she steps out of my reach and takes her hands out of my hair.

She lifts her jersey over her head and throws it to the

floor. For a moment she stands there in her thin wife-beater and sports bra before kicking off her tennis shoes and jeans.

"Pink or Blue?" she asks.

"What?"

"Condom. Pink or Blue?" Ray kneels down drawing two condom wrappers for my inspection.

"Pink," I say as I stretch out on the bed again.

"You are femme," she laughs.

"I'm happy you brought protection," I say really feeling the alcohol in my system. "I'd hate to get pregnant from a one-night stand." This gains another laugh as she unbuttons my skirt, taking it down my legs. Seconds later, my panties follow.

The climate controlled air against my Brazilian wax makes me shudder. I spread my legs to welcome Ray but she doesn't move.

"Is something wrong?" I ask as I rise to my elbows.

"I wanted to look at you," she says as she takes off her wife-beater. I throw my tank top onto our growing pile of clothes.

"How do you want me?" I ask. Ray looks around the room before lowering herself between my legs. She slides her dick in slow, allowing me to feel every inch of it inside of me. I wrap my legs around her hips and my arms around her shoulders. She pulls out just as slow, but instead of sliding back in she clutches me around the waist and lifts us both off the bed. She laughs, as I scramble to stay on her body. Ray's hands move from my waist to my butt as she walks us to the bedroom wall.

"Here," she says. "I want you here." Before I can respond, Ray thrusts inside me, the angle of her dick striking my G-spot.

"Oh my, you're strong." The words fall from my lips somehow.

"Conditioning," she grunts.

"Um...I bite," I moan as my nails dig into her shoulder blade. Ray angles her head, offering the tender flesh of her neck. I clamp down, alternating between tongue and teeth while her heavy breathing buzzes in my ear.

Finally, she stops thrusting, leaning against the wall. She takes one of her hands from my bottom and uses it to hold us up. When she catches her breath she lifts me off her dick. Even though I am still holding her shoulders, my feet stumble, so much so that she must hold me up.

"Where's your bathroom?" she asks as we lean against the wall. I nod in its direction. As Ray releases me I crumble to the floor like a jointless doll. Ray walks to the bathroom unclasping her dick. Even the nerves in my toes tingle, as I sit on the carpet.

Ray returns from the bathroom dick in hand. She kneels beside the pile of clothes looking for her pants.

"Do you want me to walk you out?" I ask.

"I didn't think we were finished?" she says as she draws something out of her pocket. She kneels down beside me planting a deep kiss on my lips. Her tongue is just as aggressive as her dick as it takes control of my mouth. She draws me into her arms where her hand unclasps my bra with the precision of a seasoned frat boy. Ray tosses the bra to the floor and her mouth forgets mine and takes to my nipples with the same urgency. My fingers tangle in her short brown hair before reaching for the edge of her wife beater. Ray pulls out of my grasp once again.

"Ray?" I try to sit up beside her only to be nudged back down. Another package rips and her head disappears between my legs. "Ray?" Her fingertips press firmly against my thighs spreading them farther. The heat of her breath between my legs has me reaching for the carpet. "What was that?

"Dental dam," she says before her tongue finds my clit.

"Are...are you always so well prepared?" I say between gasps as she works my body again in the same night. She rises once, displaying her amazing blue eyes.

"I told you I wanted to get laid," she says with a wink before disappearing.

AMSTERDAM
JULES TORTI

THIS IS THE SOUNDTRACK. The June breeze warm and friendly tickling the leaves of the towering trees outside the open window. There's a quiet whir of spinning bicycle tires along the cobblestone, the gentle lap of the wake from small wooden boats as they purr through the canal, relaxed footsteps and laughter on the sidewalk below. Doves gathering at the windowsill as dusk thickens into night.

Martine ran her fingers along Sam's butterscotch skin, her body looked so tanned against her white ribbed tank top. The weather in Holland had been unseasonably balmy, encouraging them to spend many lazy days basking in the sun like turtles, stretching out on a blanket tucked away from the busy bicycle paths of Vondelpark. Bikes and scooters delivering pizza zoomed by, walkers, runners, and happy dogs trotted by, noses to the ground. Frisbees sailed in the air with soccer balls, couples meandered hand in hand with dripping ice-cream cones, lovers passed with bottles of wine and breadsticks, looking for the perfect, hidden blanket space. Despite the constant traffic of strollers and horses and bladers, all was peaceful. To Martine, this was bliss.

They drank warm cans of Heineken, and stole surreptitious kisses in between passersby. Then, ignoring those same passersby, gazing into each other's eyes trancelike, Sam slipped her hand higher on Martine's thigh. They knew what would unfold later, back in the privacy of the hotel. Champagne, deep massages with silky oil, feeding each other blood red cherries as big as golf balls. Sam's strong, wide hand on Martine's skin made her throb and ache for those fingers on her softest flesh. She knew Sam would be wet, and she was desperate to feel that wetness on her tongue.

Sam lit a tightly rolled joint and tossed her head back with a slow exhale. They stretched out on their backs watching the clouds transform between the tree canopies. Martine marveled at the contrast of the impossibly blue sky with fingers of lush green-leafed branches poking intrusively into it. Slyly, Martine ran her fingers along the buckle of Sam's belt.

"Talk dirty to me. Tell me how you're going to fuck

me back at the hotel. Tell me what vulnerable position I'll be in," Martine whispered.

"Mmm, I always love you on your stomach, babe, sliding against your hard ass, especially when you're all slippery with massage oil."

"Will you be touching yourself while you do this sliding thing?" Martine asked.

"Sometimes I just want to feel you. I like that thrill of no hands, for a little bit at least. I like pushing into you from behind, and feeling the bones of your low back against my swollen clit. Just imagining that I'm inside you is such a turn-on."

"Anytime you're ready to go back to the hotel and, you know, try those awful, torturous things on me. Besides, it looks like a storm might blow up," Martine pointed out, not very convincingly as the sun beat down on their bodies.

"Nice try on the storm front, babe. But, I suppose if you're nervous about a thunderstorm, we should take cover. Immediately." Sam slipped her tongue inside Martine's mouth, making the hot ache between her legs consume her mind in a dizzy fever of naked thoughts.

Sam passed her the roach clip as Martine stroked the tribal armband on Sam's perfectly sculpted deltoid. She always admired Sam's muscles, how a body so powerfully built with thick biceps and a wide back from a punishing gym routine, could be so soft and gentle against hers.

"Back to the hotel?" Sam asked, unable to contain herself either. Martine nodded yes with the enthusiasm of a dog knowing it was going for a w-a-l-k.

They folded the picnic blanket like a difficult map, stumbling and giggling as they bumped heads in their rush. Martine packed away the postcards they had yet to write, and the heavily highlighted, dog-eared copy of *Lonely Planet*. The small Dutch language guidebook from her mother had yet to be opened.

Hand in hand, Martine and Sam walked along the Leidesplein, past the stately American Hotel, the strip of theaters, and the Cox café with espresso drinking patrons spilling out onto the narrow sidewalk. They headed in the direction of the Titus Hotel, speeding along faster than usual with the anticipation of peeling each other's clothes off and falling into the bed.

Martine bounded up the steep staircase of Titus, snickering about the events of the night before. They had drunk bottles of Shiraz on the boat cruise through the canals with a straight couple from Wales, and staggered through the Red Light district with dripping chicken shawarmas together. They even convinced Jared and Allison to smoke skunky Thai pot at the Bulldog; it was their first wedding anniversary, after all! Later, Sam lost her sandals on the way up the steep stairs of the hotel, and somehow she lost her top too.

Sam had surprised Martine with the plane tickets to Amsterdam. She had wrapped the tickets cleverly, in a picnic basket with a wheel of smoked Gouda and a six-pack of Heineken. She had a bike courier deliver them to Martine's downtown office. "Meet me after work at Slack's to discuss details and appropriate footwear. P.S. I already asked your boss for the time off. Love, Sam xoxo". Three days later they were walking from Central Station, sipping strong European coffee, and sharing a sugary *appleflak* on the steps of the van Gogh museum. Sam had a meeting with a brewing company just west of Amsterdam at the beginning of the week, and a promotional gig at two of the popular gay bars, April and the COC. The rest of the week would be theirs to explore and wander.

Arriving back at the room, after another lazy day at Vondelpark, they quickly pulled the king bed to the large open window, so they could watch the activity on the canal. As night fell, the lights from the boats would twinkle like blurred candle wicks and fireflies. The moon would soon be anchored above the sloping architecture of Marnixstraat. The light from the streetlamps along the canal in front of the Titus Hotel would flood softly into the room, casting a buttery glow on their naked bodies

A young shirtless guy with shaggy hair and baggy cargos picked at his guitar on the park bench beneath their window. A thin girl in long beaded dreads in a sundress beside him licked ice cream from a waffle cone, and tucked her bare feet underneath his legs. The park bench was a constant fluid transition of faces, mostly lovelorn, some lost or weary, others relaxed and daydreamy. From the window, Sam and Martine had their secret view of their own private Amsterdam.

Martine's heart pounded wildly in her ribcage now that she and Sam were alone. Her blood zoomed through her raised veins in excited loops. Sam had already lit dozens of tea lights in the darkened corners and smiled devilishly at Martine. She expertly opened the chilled champagne but overflowed the first glass with a laugh. Martine unpacked the bag from the deli around the corner, and spread the makeshift picnic on the bed. Sam overflowed the second glass and proposed a sticky toast. The glasses were soon abandoned for kisses, and shirts and shorts were pulled off as the heat between their bodies intensified. Anyone looking up at the second floor would have enjoyed quite the show. Two women, lips and tongues dragging across stiff nipples, sharing lusty kisses with a hungry force. They laughed at their nakedness in front of the window, somewhat anticipating the thrill of being spotted. Sam playfully pushed Martine onto the bed, causing the plastic container of spicy olives to tip and roll about.

Sam loved to play with Martine's hair, smoothing down the blonde spikes that would only pop back up again. She ran her finger along the back of her neck, where her hair was shorter, like the soft bristles of a kiwi. Martine rolled to her side, pulling Sam's body close. She popped an olive in Sam's mouth and watched her take in the length of her finger.

Sam cut thin slices of Gouda with her jackknife, and fed Martine generous pieces of pillowy baguette with the cheese. They took turns feeding each other marinated olives, tender crab legs, and cherry tomatoes stuffed with goat's cheese. Sam licked Martine's fingers like she was licking her swollen clit.

There was something about Sam that mesmerized Martine. Maybe it was the way she vividly described the full body massage she would be giving her later. Her words were almost a whisper, and she spoke with the glass of champagne close to her lips. Just as Martine would be eager to hear more, Sam would purposely take a sip and grin. She teased Martine with words often, and deliberately didn't touch Martine when she spoke, knowing that was what she craved. Sam created precise visual movies of what she was going to do to Martine, and at the height of the frenzy she put her in, Sam would finally touch her. That first touch would be so overwhelming, like a plunge into the Atlantic, leaving Martine nearly gasping, goose bumps racing across her skin.

Martine loved to watch the movie spin in Sam's eyes. They were brown like the shell of Brazil nuts and dark Quebec maple syrup. Her carefully plucked eyebrows raised a little, and she could arch the left one exactly like a scolding teacher. When she wore her blue tinted sunglasses, Martine waited for the moment when Sam would lower her chin and look above the frames of the glasses with her eyebrows up a little. There was something tremendously sexy about that, and it was something she only did when she spoke to Martine.

Pushing the picnic aside, Martine rolled Sam over onto her stomach, and coaxed her easily to her knees, Sam's favorite position. Martine loved pushing her pelvis into Sam's muscular ass. She would almost climax herself when Sam would go from quietly lying on her stomach, to her knees, spreading her legs wide for Martine. She would just open right up to Martine's touch, and beg in a whisper to be teased around her ass. Martine would tease her with one slow hand, sliding into the soft folds of Sam's delicate skin, feeling her hard clit pop out on her fingertips. They would happily trade hand positions and Sam would touch herself, rhythmically, then with a quick vibration that traveled though to Martine, which aroused her even more.

Tonight though, Martine needed to kiss Sam in those soft, wet folds of her pussy, to feel her pink labia soft on her tongue. Martine turned Sam over, and Sam laughed at her indecisive mind. Martine made a quick trail from Sam's tight knot of a navel to her inner thighs with her tongue. She admired the beauty before her, like a van Gogh that deserved silence and deep reflection. Sam's fine dark hairs were trimmed short, her glistening lips the color of ripe damson plums. Sam propped herself up on a pillow and pulled the thin sheet over Martine's head as the breeze cooled. She watched intently from under the sheet as Martine slid her tongue around in her wetness, flickering her tongue like the beat of a hummingbird's wings.

The feathery contact excited Sam and left her urgent for more. She pulled at Martine's short hair, desperate to have her closer and harder on her clit. Martine pushed her hips into the wet spot on the mattress, gyrating her hips as though Sam's body was underneath her. She skimmed her hand over Sam's hard stomach and reached for her firm breasts. The milky tan lines of Sam's breasts were lighter than the bronzed skin of her freckled chest and stomach. Martine tugged her dark nipples just hard enough to give her that electric feeling she craved.

Sam spread her legs further. The taste of Sam was so familiar in Martine's mouth. She licked faster as Sam encouraged her with quick thrusts of her pelvis. Martine teased her ass again with slippery K-Y, and slipped in slightly, gingerly, in and out, matching the rhythm of her tongue. Sam smiled her crooked smile and let her head fall briefly back onto the pillow. They loved having eye contact, watching each other, enjoying the sensations expressed in each other's eyes.

Putting her smooth heels on Martine's shoulders, Sam opened up even further, begging for more penetration. She dug her heels in as Martine entered her further, deep against her G-spot, with two fingers slid into her ass. Martine couldn't believe her own wetness on the sheets, as her left hand traced Sam's curves, and grabbed her muscular quads. She tickled her fine treasure line, and the tiny strip of hair above her pussy.

A slick of sweat formed in the arch of Martine's back, and on her forehead as she kept up with Sam's quick momentum. She teased her, pushed deep into her, and spoke in a syrupy voice about the thoughts of having a strap-on, and thrusting it into Sam's warm walls. She held onto her hips, watching the tattoo on the inside of her hip bone jump as her muscles contracted. Sam slid her finger into Martine's warm mouth, feeling the texture of her tongue, firm against her.

Martine rode slowly, in and out of Sam's ass, that tight little ass that she fantasized about at work as she stared out from fifty-six floors above downtown Toronto. That ass that she could see through the bulk of her hockey pants and padding. In the arena stands, sipping a tall hot chocolate, Martine had Sam stripped down to her jock, on her knees on the goal line, penetrating that hockey ass. *Two minutes for roughing.*

Sam's breathing was becoming more rapid, she pulled at Martine's hair harder, she was close. Martine pushed in and out of her ass, and watched as Sam's hand pulled back her lips, exposing her swolen clit. Sam's fingers moved across her own clit fast. Martine loved when Sam made herself come. "I'm going to, I'm gonna come," Sam breathed.

Martine felt the rush, the clenching of muscles around her fingers, the wetness that spilled out as she came. Sam's body shuddered and jumped, relaxing and contracting as her breath slowed. Gentle with her tongue, Martine caressed her Sam's clit. She crawled up on top of Sam's body, kissing all the inches from her navel to her loving lips, salty with sweat. Sam hugged her close, their breasts pressing together. She tucked the sheet in tight around them.

They listened to the June breeze, the quiet whir of bicycles, the lulling lap of the wake, distant laughter, footsteps, and their breathing. Sam's breath, deep and heavy, and Martine's breath, slowing to match Sam's. They finished the last of the champagne, and a few ripe cherries with pieces of Dutch chocolate, silently watching the canal. They admired the world passing outside their window, and embraced the world inside the window, inside each other's arms.

SCARS

JESI O'CONNELL

SHOW ME YOUR BACK.

Why?

Just do it.

Her voice is still soft, as always. It reminds me of a butterfly tickling against my skin, or a ladybug gently exploring the valleys and peaks of my hand, my small fingers. There is no demand in her words, no command, no hurry. Yet something in that soft tone has me turning around, a bolt of sheer lightning zipping down my spine to nestle directly between my legs. My naked skin twitches and ripples as if a real butterfly is crossing it, rather than the innocuous, intangible flow of words from my sweet lover.

Mm.

That little sound, less a word than a sigh, comes right from her core. It wraps around me, lazy, gentle, tiptoeing as if to avoid startling me. There is a rush of moisture in my own core, an abrupt dryness in my mouth.

Your back—

I interrupt her before the end of that sentence can shatter the moment.

It doesn't hurt. It never hurts. It just looks—wounded. My voice is bright.

It was wounded, once upon a time. Her voice is still soft, yet also clinical, detached in a nonjudgmental way. I relax. A little. *May I look at it?*

A tiny silence cocoons us. My back feels so exposed, so—beyond naked. Vulnerable. I let my head drift down toward my chest, my eyes closing. Dark hair, loosened from its clasps, slips around my face. The excitement is still with me, dancing around my thighs, caressing my breasts. So is the fear.

I breathe deeply in, out, in. My yoga teacher has us practice breathing every session, tells us to do it at home too. He says it will calm me when I am stressed, or tired, or sore, or even a bit panicked. Does this moment count as panic?

Breathe, she says, and I realize that I released all the air in my lungs and forgot to take more in. I gulp in a huge burst of air. And as I do, I feel her hand on my back, lightly touching me, tracing the scars, feeling the map of me on my skin.

Do you believe me?

Believe you what?

When I touch you.

My skin ripples at her words. Her light fingers outline my back.

Do you believe me when I touch you? Do you believe that I want to touch you? That you do not scare me?

I cannot answer her.

Then I will just have to keep proving myself to you.

Both her hands are on my back now. She is still tracing and also beginning to knead, just a bit, carefully rolling her fingers over me. She finds the big scar, the ropy one that passes over my shoulder blade and curls around my spine like a thick lashing tail, and pauses over it for an eternity. The scar seems to intensify, become heated, under her touch. It is an impossible sensation.

This is agonizing, I manage to stutter out in a voice that is not mine.

This is beautiful.

You are nuts. I don't sound convincing.

You are astonishing.

I am speechless.

If I touch you here, and she leaves one hand on the big scar, *and also here,* and suddenly her other hand is fluttering between my legs, her nails lightly trailing against my labia, one finger tapping on my rear, *how will you react, I wonder?*

I am gasping. I try to breathe. My yoga teacher is not winning this one. My chest is heaving up and down, the sounds coming out of my mouth are not quite pretty, definitely not graceful. My clitoris abruptly has a mind of its own, sneaky little thing, and shoots more mini lightning bolts out along my nerve endings.

Urrgghh-ummm, is what I come up with. She leans against my back, trapping her one hand between us. Some of her hair, Little Orphan Annie orange, drapes over my shoulder to mix with my dark strands. We are the same height. Her body matches mine to a perfect degree, like those little Russian dolls that fit inside one another, nestling together. I can feel her laughter bubbling up, echoing against me, shaking me the way it shakes her. It is as if we two are one, sharing an emotion in a blended body.

I thought so. Don't move for a minute, hmm? I want to keep exploring you.

Movement is not possible. My legs are beginning to tremble, just a bit. Not from exhaustion—from a need. I need her to let me lie down. I need to be on my back, exposing the rest of me to her. I need to hide and yet offer myself up simultaneously.

She moves away from me again, one hand still on my broken, rippled skin, the other playing between my legs like I am a piano, a violin, a keyboard. With her hand she is creating masterpieces. I try to stifle a moan but it escapes. Just a little one, but she hears it in the unnaturally quiet room.

Ah-ha, is all she says. Her voice is smug, the cat that got the cream. Her fingers do not stop. I can picture her nails, neat, manicured, painted with just a touch of glistening pink, politely nudging at my clit, gliding over it. The nails on my back have smoothly traced and retraced all my scars, connected them, run across them like they are roads leading to perilous yet exquisite adventure.

My skin is beginning to tingle, just a little bit. The soft, full skin of my labia, swelling just the smallest bit, quivers with anticipation. The skin on my back, raised into the ugly deep red welts, has sensation whispering over it with a promise.

My scars do not have sensation. The doctors told me they never will.

My skin murmurs to me that doctors do not know everything. They especially do not know how my lover touches me.

More. I almost do not recognize the slightly cracking voice as my own.

What?

More. Please.

She dances her fingers over me, moving from a waltz to a cha-cha in the blink of an eye. It is so sudden, so intense, that I cry out.

You can't take more. Not yet. Not until later.

The movement slows back to a bearable pace. I can feel heat coiling inside me like a serpent, deep inside my belly, winding and unwinding down toward my pubic bone and below. It moves slowly, unhurried despite my mind's urgings.

What if I can?

You can't. The butterfly voice is sure, implacable, soft and insistent. She trails one finger up my crack, gently teasing my ass. My skin sizzles and I feel that rush and start, like someone is pouring cool water over me. It raises my nerves endings into shock and protest and a delicious anticipation. She laughs.

Her fingers thrum against my skin, dipping inside me, twirling in my wetness. I envision a rainbow being swirled with ice cream, the sky tilting around me, the slow build of the roller coaster car heading up the big hill, the one right before the long screaming whistle of a drop.

Yes, that's right, she says. I hear my voice then, a little whimper with panting, unintelligible words. My body leans forward. I want to collapse now; I want to fall to the ground, to the fluffy mound of canary-yellow and tomato-red pillows and patchwork down comforters she has created into a little nest in the middle of the bare floor for just this purpose.

She holds me up, keeps me with her. The hand on my back winds around to the front, palm flat against my belly.

Ah ah ah. Her voice chides like a preschool teacher scolding the child who has her hand in the cookie jar before lunch. *I want you standing up. Just like this.*

I—can't. Not like this. Labored, a touch aggrieved. I am pouting.

Oh, yes, you can. You will.

Oh. Well, in that case.

Her hands are firm, her arms, indeed her whole body, incredibly strong for being so small. It has always been my lament that I, too, am short and small. I thought it made me weak, helpless and open to the whim of others.

She quickly disabused me of that notion when we met. She is the strongest person I know. Delicate smile, crazy wild orange hair, little stick arms and legs. The kind of woman people sometimes mistake for a child until she turns around and holds them with those piercing grown-up eyes. She can hold me with a single word or glance. She can hold me because I let her, because I want her to. She is teaching me that I am helpless only if I allow myself to be.

I am aware of her breasts, little globes of pure sensitivity, pressing against my ragged back. They are so soft, and I know my back is not. For a second, I tense.

Don't. Her voice is so gentle I almost miss it.

Stay with me. I like the way you feel.

One perfect little nail pushes inside me, all the way to the knuckle joint. She moves the finger around in me, like a little electric beater—first one way, then the other. Once again, I make unintelligible sounds. Once again, she emits a little giggle. Another finger follows the first.

Stay still. I want to feel everything inside you. I want to feel each ridge of flesh. I want to feel you tighten around my fingers. I want your juices to run down my hand. And then I want to taste my fingers.

I am beyond complaining.

Here. To the wall. Brace against it. Butterfly voice again. Not to be disobeyed. We sort of shuffle toward the wall, clambering over the pile of pillows and down. I put my hands up and touch the wall. I push my palms into the glossy paint over the little textured bumps. My fingers curl against the wall's coolness before pressing flat, hard.

Look at my hand. She takes the hand on my stomach away and slides it down to join the other, accompanied by a slightly strangled gasp from me. *Look at my fingers disappearing inside you. I want you to see what is making you feel so exquisite. Look.*

I tuck my head down again and see her hand against my thighs, over my pussy, fingers trailing over my clitoris, swollen with blood and need and the some lingering, mild panic. Her chest still pushes into my back. Every now and then I can feel her nipples, hard as little pebbles, randomly rubbing my scars as if they are fingers. The feeling excites me more, in a primal, almost ashamed manner. My scarred, ugly back as erogenous zone. If it didn't feel so delicious, I would laugh at the joke.

As it is, I can only try to match my rough breath to her movements against me, inside me. Her tongue flicks out, licks my ear, and I jerk away momentarily before coming back under her mouth like a cat wanting its head rubbed.

Good girl. Is that a purr?

I can see my hair and hers, mingling together, making a teasing screen over the sight of her hands. One finger is now exploring the folds of my labia, except that they are no longer folds. They are plump little regions of pleasure, of nearly agonizing sensation. Another finger, her index by its strength and precision, has excavated my clitoris between the sheltering fat labia and is brushing it with little finger kisses. My own moisture lubricates her skilled hands. I can feel myself dripping down my legs.

Aah-uhh. Articulation has left me. I can feel her smile against my ear, an approving exhale of breath. Her tongue still plays with the curves and wrinkles of my ear, the strokes and explorations matching her fingers between my legs.

Let the wall hold you. I need to readjust.

With a quick grace, she slides one leg across me, anchoring herself around me. My left leg, thrust behind me for balance, now supports her. I can feel her straddling me close, her own slick wetness nuzzling my leg. Her breasts still dance and glide over my ravaged back.

I do not have to hear her sigh. I feel it echoing in my bones, vibrating throughout me, spinning down to that one spot, the one she is cajoling and playing and teasing with her fingers/tongue, the spot that is beginning to swallow me, becoming my entire body, unable to distinguish between ear and clit, back and breasts, me and her.

There you go.

How does she keep her voice steady?

There we go.

Three fingers are inside me now, pushing insistently, twirling around like little ballerinas inside my wet cunt. A beautiful rush is spinning me. I look at the hand that seems almost taken whole by me. Suddenly, she removes it, and I almost cry from the loss.

She puts her fingers into her mouth. I can hear her elegantly slurping at them, making gracious little murmurs of pleasure as she does. My entire cunt constricts, throbs, as I hear her licking my juices off her hand.

Taste.

Her hand is in my mouth. I taste myself. I am delectable, tangy, that incomparable sex smell on my taste buds, flooding my mouth.

She pulls away from me, just a bit. Her hand comes

up and rubs my back, drawing my scars with fingers that smell and taste like me. My back tingles and shudders. Another moan escapes me. I make no effort to hide it. A throaty laugh tangles with her hair, her tongue back in my ear, her hand back on my mound, her fingers easily, so easily slipping back inside me.

Another advantage to being small, and now her voice is a whisper. I can hear it beginning to break, just a bit. *I can fit my whole hand inside you—like—so.*

I am rigid with amazed, billowing shock. I can see her hand slide into me, engulfed by my puffed-out lips, my sweat-slicked thighs, covered by the little bristle of dark curly hairs. I am tight yet loose. My muscles hold her close inside me. I think I can feel every knob on each one of her fingers in the neat little packet of her hand sucked into the greedy, wet darkness that is me.

Let me in.

She is moving against my leg, gently shifting back and forth, up and down. Slowly, with infinite precision, she lets herself slip lower down so that her lips are on my back. Her hands have more dexterity on me, in me, now. She uses them. I am being penetrated to my depths. Her hand is slightly twisting inside me. Her fingers create little currents on my inner flesh, like shadows of spiraling need, flashes of hot white light pulsing in me.

I inhale. Exhale.

Breathe. Must not panic.

Inhale. Exhale.

Her lips are traveling across my back, leaving little wet marks that raise goose bumps from an oddly languorous zip of desire. I feel her lips pause, nibble at the big ropy scar. My back spasms, automatically arching away from her, but I am met by the wall. I cannot escape.

Stay with me. She sounds a little more ragged, like a prim debutante whose top has started to slip down her shoulders, exposing more than is acceptable of her swelling chest. But her words are still solid, almost ferocious in their need. *I need you to believe me.*

Her fingers twitch inside me. The talented one on my clitoris is revolving around, around, lighting sparks in the center of her touch, on the sides, in each millimeter of sweetly bruised flesh. The low, unstoppable thrumming begins, deep inside. Her touch is raising a tiger, a wild clawing want. A surfacing want in me.

Her mouth chews at me. Her tongue slides along a scar, kissing, nibbling. Tasting me.

I—

Breathe.

Yes. Her voice is a ragged purr in the hollow of my back.

I—

Deeply.

I know.

She does know. The tiger is spiraling out of me. She is sliding herself along my leg with a regular motion. Her fingers stroke, tease, twirl inside me. I can feel a spurt of warmth, of wetness inside me slicking her fingers, her hand, coating her with my longing. I can feel her moving against me, with me, on me, around me. Her lips kiss my scars. My ruined flesh twitches as if a thousand stars are shooting into it. I arch my back toward her.

My need rises in a huge rush, starting right under her finger on my clit and exploding out to the sides, down my rubbery legs, straight up my belly, spreading across my back in that glitter of star shower. I throw my head back and howl with the tiger in me.

She howls too, hot wetness soaking the back of my leg where she rides. Her unrestrained noise is still, like the rest of her, oddly dainty. I shake, and shake, and shake. I am not dainty. I am not controlled.

I breathe. My breaths are wobbly, but they take in air.

She breathes with me, in and out, matching gasp for gasp. My tremors have not yet subsided when she carefully lets us drop, finally, to the soft nest she has made. My hands leave sweat as they trail down the wall and gently thump to the ground.

The room is still but for the rustle of material pulled over skin, the shifting of limbs. It smells pungent. Spicy. Satisfied.

Turn over.

I comply and lie beneath her, looking into her eyes. They are an unfocused soft green. They look right at me. Right into me.

She strokes first one of my eyebrows, then the other, with a fingertip. I can smell myself on her. Her face is serious. I stretch my arms around her, pull her closer, not taking my gaze from hers.

I take a deep breath. My voice is steady.

I believe.

THE GO-TO GAL
TERESA NOELLE ROBERTS

EVERY GROUP OF FRIENDS has a go-to guy or gal, the one who fixes things, the one who takes care of people, the one you can turn to, no matter how weird the problem, knowing it will be solved.

The one you take for granted will be there for you.

In our crowd, that's Delia.

Delia's a big woman, six feet tall and over two hundred muscular pounds, with short-cropped fair hair and the broad-cheeked, pointy-chinned face of a housecat, including the slanted, lazily observant green eyes. She can fix just about anything, from a lawn mower to a sewing machine to your car. She's the one who organizes the Food Brigade for the person who had a baby or an operation. The one you call when you need a hand with moving or with stacking firewood; when your plumbing springs a leak or your plaster starts crumbling; when you need pants shortened or the fabulous thrift-shop find altered to fit you properly; when you have to collect stuff from your creepy ex's place and you want someone with you who radiates "Don't try that shit with me!" The one who's always there for everyone else.

This time, though, the go-to gal had come to me, and as soon as she walked in my door, I knew why.

"Mallory's gone," I said. Not asked. It wasn't a question. The only questions were the details: whether Delia had been smart enough to throw her out or if she'd left on her own flaky initiative. Beautiful woman, Mallory, but all kinds of crazy. Couldn't keep a job, couldn't be faithful, couldn't tell the truth, couldn't stay sober, as if she were compelled to wreck her own life and everyone else's. Only Delia being tough and stubborn as she was had kept them together this long.

"She's on her way to Cincinnati, where her latest behind-my-back girlfriend is. I finally told her to straighten out or get out and she got out. Left all the trash behind and took Jasper. Damn it, she took Jasper." Jasper was their dog. In the long run, I figured Delia would miss that dog a lot more than she did Mallory, but that was the long run. "I can fix just about any other damn thing. But how do you fix a broken heart?"

"Your heart's been breaking for a long time now. That

woman–" I took a deep breath and searched my mental database for tact and diplomacy, examples thereof: "Has issues. It hasn't been an easy relationship."

Despite the pain on her face, Delia laughed. Not quite her usual hearty chuckle, but a laugh, anyway. "That's like saying Hurricane Katrina did a little damage. I know throwing her out was the right thing to do. I tried to help her, but I think even if she wanted to change, and she doesn't at this point, it would take professional help. She's poison for me. But Jeanne, when it was good–"

At that point Delia lost her battle to stay calm.

I pulled her in for a hug, because sometimes that's all you can do.

Funny. I'd hugged Delia many times. Always, I'd focused on her strength and size, the muscles of her arms, her broad back.

This time I noticed other things as well. Her understated scent, some floral-herbal blend I couldn't identify, but liked, layered over warm, womanly flesh heated by summer sun. The feel of her shirt, a simple rose-colored cotton tank top washed to baby softness. The velvet texture of her skin.

And her breasts. Oh God, her breasts. I'm shorter than Delia—for that matter, I'm shorter than my twelve-year-old niece—and I'd been crushed against her cleavage many times. I'd always enjoyed that, but the enjoyment was tempered by knowing that Mallory (despite the fact that she'd cheated on Delia regularly) was insanely jealous and a gun and knife collector.

Mallory and her weapons were heading west, though,

and all I could say was good riddance.

Now that I really let myself contemplate them, Delia had some of the most amazing breasts I'd ever seen, full and firm and soft. And right now, my face was pressing right up against them.

My heart started playing techno: 180 beats per minute and syncopated weirdly, but good for dancing—or sex. After a few seconds, my clit picked up the beat.

One of my hands slipped to her broad, round, denim-clad ass. The curve where butt met thigh fit perfectly into my hand.

I'd never seen Delia naked, but we'd been to the beach together, which gave me enough clues to put together a lovely picture of abundant curves over firm muscles. Beauty and strength and ripe peach nipples and thick blonde curls accenting a delicious sex.

I brushed my lips lightly over the skin under my lips, not actually her breast, but the place where "chest" starts to become "cleavage". A butterfly kiss, nothing more, but that little taste set me on fire.

Great. I was making advances at one of my best friends, who was crying in my arms because she finally dumped her crazy, cheating lover. Bad karma, that.

I forced myself to pull away. "Let me get you some tissues," I said, desperately trying to back-pedal. "Or maybe a drink. I've iced tea, beer–"

"It's all right, Jeanne. It's more than all right." Her hand closed on my wrist. Big against my finer bones, pale against my own brown skin.

Good lord, she was beautiful.

I wondered how I'd defended myself against her for so long, body and heart, and then realized I really hadn't. I just hadn't been smart enough to realize why I kept finding excuses to see her as often as I could, even when it meant seeing Psycho Mallory and her knives as well.

"It wasn't my plan, but maybe it's why I came here," Delia said. "I've cried enough over that woman. And they say loving well is the best revenge."

Living well, I thought. *The line is living well.*

Then she reeled me in and kissed me.

Living well, loving well. Same thing, right? Works for me, anyway.

Sweat beaded on our skin as we kissed and kissed, and ran our hands anywhere we could reach. I was almost climbing her when she cupped my ass with both hands and lifted me off the floor.

I wrapped my legs around her hips, moving against her. Her hands supported me effortlessly. Awkward, but hot.

"Bedroom?" Delia asked.

"Bedroom!"

She carried me there as if I were a child. Kicked the half-closed door open, startling my cat off the bed. Dropped me onto the tangles of the unmade bed and threw herself down beside me. I let myself spend half a second regretting that I hadn't changed the sheets, which were rather the worse for cat hair and a few hot (in the 90-degree and high humidity sense) nights.

Then I slipped my hands under the hem of her tank top, working it up as I explored the soft curve of her belly, velvet padding over the hard muscles of her core. Kisses for that beauty, and extra kisses because I'd heard Mallory mock her roundness, and never mind that Delia was actually fit and Mallory was just skinny.

I worked the top up until she sat up a bit and wriggled out of it.

A white cotton bra patterned with pale pink hearts— like Delia, both practical and sweet. Her nipples, darker than I'd envisioned, showed through the thin fabric, rosy-brown and fat and tempting.

I ran my fingers over them, was rewarded by a shudder of pleasure. Did it again and again until they were straining against the white and pink knit, swelling deliciously outward, demanding more attention. Then I cupped more of the sweet flesh in my hands, clasped the nipples in a soft squeeze, rolled them teasingly.

"Oh, yeah!" she breathed.

I suckled through the fabric, first one nipple, then the other, caressing the one that wasn't in my mouth. I loved feeling their firmness under my tongue, loved feeling and hearing Delia react. But the delicate barrier between me and them was driving me nuts. Time for the bra to go.

It did. We took the opportunity to get rid of the rest of our clothes. She ran her hands over me, breasts and ass and thighs. Fire followed them. I was throbbing with anticipation.

But—and maybe it was odd, but it was what I was feeling—it was more the anticipation of touching her, making her scream, seeing her shatter and come back together. Sometimes it really is better to give than to receive, or at least just as good in a different way. "You first," I said, pushing her back down gently with a hand planted in the middle of her chest. "I want to spoil you."

Under my hand, she moved like a pleased cat stretching in the sun. "I could use a little spoiling," she conceded, "but I'll want to return the favor."

"Once you catch your breath."

I almost laughed at how confident I sounded. I'd heard from roughly half the dykes in the area what a hot ticket Mallory was, what a store of kinky sex-tricks she had up her sleeve—usually right before they added, "too bad she's completely insane." But I figured there was a lot to be said for patience, persistence, and attention to detail. And, for that matter, for giving a damn about your partner as a person, not just a distraction against the noise in your head. There, I'd have the advantage.

Delia's breasts were even lovelier than I'd imagined, pale and lightly freckled except for the dark, plump nipples, and they settled into my hands as if they trusted me. And the rest of her body matched their glory, lush and succulent and gloriously female. I could smell more of that perfume of hers, more light sweat, and underneath it all a hint of the fragrance of desire. I felt small next to her, small yet privileged, as if I'd been chosen to make love to a goddess.

"I already suspected Mallory was nuts," I murmured over one delicious breast. "Seeing you like this proves it. No sane woman would run around when she could come home to this."

Delia laughed, really laughed, this time, although

there was regret behind it as well. "Never said she was sane, did I?"

And then I bit down gently on the nipple and turned the laugh into another kind of noise.

Suckled and nibbled until she was squirming and panting and the room sang with the smell of her need.

Kissed my way down her body, but made myself not go directly to her pussy. Delia must have been neglected, half-loved, for a long time. I couldn't make up for all of it in one afternoon, but damn it, I could make a valiant effort.

Kisses for her thighs, both the muscled outside and the delicate, silken inside. Kisses for the calves, because no one ever thinks to kiss those. Kisses down to the ankles. I lavished attention on her feet as well, until she started squirming away and giggling, "Too much! Too much!"

Then I worked my way back up her legs and rested my head against the golden curls, spent a few seconds just drinking in her rich scent, that ocean-goddess smell that pushed my own body into overdrive. "Please," she begged, and I snaked out my tongue, teasing at her mound, but not touching where she needed me. "Please," she begged again, and that time I couldn't resist.

I shifted between her legs, opened her up a little more, plunged in my tongue

She was juicy and sweet as a ripe plum, and she cried out at the first lick, not from orgasm yet, but surprise and joy.

I began to devour her.

Just tongue at first, licking the juices off her slick lips, swirling around her clit, loving how swollen it was, and much more swollen and eager it got under my attention.

I gave her the first orgasm that way.

And when she was still twitching from that, I started working my fingers inside her.

First one, then two, curving up to tease at the spongy, sensitive G-spot while I kept licking away. An electric jolt passed through her, and she clamped down on my fingers, fluttering hard against them, her cunt as strong as the rest of her.

I let Delia rest then, but only long enough to find lube in my dresser drawer.

I have a few tricks of my own.

One of them involves the fact I'm a small woman. Small bones. Small, flexible hands. Hey, we all work with what we have.

When the first couple of fingers went in, she just purred. The third made her writhe. The fourth caused her to beat her fist on the mattress and gasp my name.

When I worked in my thumb as well, her eyes widened. "So full," she said, and her voice was quiet with awe. I moved gently in and out, letting her open up and get used to the sensation, trying to make her feel, but not yet make her come.

"I've never—" Her voice faltered. "I need...please."

"I know. And I know what you need." Awkwardly, I squirted a little more lube onto the bit of my hand that was still exposed. "I'll take you there. I'll take care of you, darling." I was a little surprised she'd never done this with Mallory, or anyone else, but thrilled, too.

She was tightening from excitement, contracting around me.

"Breathe for me. Try to relax. I'll take my time." I curled my hand in on itself lengthwise, making it narrower, worked gently.

"Too much!" Delia exclaimed, and then, almost instantly, "Not too much. Good."

In a process gradual and beautiful as a sunrise, I found myself inside her, surrounded by her, my wrist holding her lips wide, my fist rocking inside her tight walls. She was talking still, but it had broken down to happy babbling.

And I was babbling right back at her, telling her how slick and hot she felt, how wonderful it was to be inside her, how proud I was to be the first woman to do this to her, how incredibly beautiful she looked with her face red and contorted with lust and her body beaded with sweat. Only that makes it sound a lot more coherent than it was, because I was having a kind of mental orgasm myself. I hadn't dared to touch myself for fear I'd get distracted and hurt Delia, but the fact that the usual parts of my body weren't in play didn't seem to matter. My brain was ready to explode, seeing Delia impaled on my hand, and so was my cunt.

All it would take would be to feel her contract around my whole hand.

"Will you come for me now?" I whispered.

When she nodded, I flicked one finger of my other hand across her clit and made sure of it.

The noise she made wasn't human, and she tightened

and spasmed so much I was sure, with my two function-
ing brain cells, that one or both of us would end up with
the kind of injury it's embarrassing to explain at the ER.

Then I echoed her, and the world went nova-bright.

When my eyes focused again, I realized Delia was
crying. No hysterical sobs or anything, but tears were
streaming quietly down her face.

Nevertheless, she was beaming.

I wasn't sure what to make of that. So, being an occasionally sensible person, I asked, "Are you okay?"

She blinked away the tears. "Better than I have been in
a while. I can't remember–" More tears, just a few, and I
kissed them away. "I can't remember the last time someone took such good care of me. And I don't just mean in
bed. I mean–"

Light dawned. "You mean you're the one who takes
care of everyone else. Mallory, of course, but we all call
on you whenever we need help, and you're always there
for us. But you seem so self-sufficient, so strong. Even
with Mallory. Anyone else would have dumped her—or
killed her—a long time ago, but you acted like everything
was fine and we figured you had it under control until
the very end."

I realized I was ranting, took a deep breath. "So what
I'm trying to say is I'm sorry, for not realizing you might
need help too."

"Nothing to apologize for." She pulled me close. "But
even caregivers need someone to take care of them
sometimes."

"I'll volunteer!" I said, way too eagerly. Then I amended

it to, "I mean in general... not like this, unless–" God, she was going to think I'd be showing up with the proverbial moving van, and really, it was a little soon for that—even though I could think of far worse eventual outcomes.

"What's wrong with like this?" Delia said. "I like this. Just as long as I get to take care of you too."

And then she rolled over, pinning me to the bed, and proceeded to demonstrate something I already knew: that she was very good with her hands and very, very good at taking care of others.

COVERING
TENILLE BROWN

I LAY CLOSE TO Charlotte in bed, pressed firmly against her long, lean body. It didn't matter that we were in the middle of the hottest month of the year and that it was quite possibly the hottest night; the feel of her near me made the muggy heat and the sweat that made my clothes stick to me all worthwhile.

I lifted my bare leg and lay it across her hip. I rubbed my thigh against hers, the friction of my skin against hers causing a warm sensation that traveled from the top of my knee across the hill that was my hip to the base of my belly. My knee rested comfortably in the deep cave behind hers.

Charlotte reached up and covered my hand with her own and gently squeezed, locking her fingers between mine. She pulled my hand tighter around her middle, tucking it beneath her cropped T-shirt. Then she lowered it so that it rested against the soft fabric of her cotton panties. I leaned in and nuzzled her neck, inhaling the lingering sweetness that mingled with the thin veil of perspiration that rested on her berry skin.

Fueled by Charlotte's reaction, I became bold. I placed my bare foot against hers and rubbed slowly, the cotton of her socks soft against my sole.

I became bolder still. I gently tucked my toe beneath the ridges of her sock, so that my foot rested against her exposed ankle. Then she was suddenly still. Charlotte's grip on my hand loosened, causing it to fall limply against her thigh. I stopped moving as well. I took my foot away from hers, pulled my hand away and sighed.

It had become a routine, a silent dance that took place in the middle of our bed on nights when I couldn't control myself, when there seemed to be a magnetic pull that I couldn't fight against.

Always, always I was drawn to her feet and always, they were hidden by a pair of socks. It didn't matter how cold or how hot it was, Charlotte wore them like masks, covering her size elevens as if they were scarred.

"I just want to rub them a little," I said in my softest voice, "just for a minute. You don't even have to take the socks off if you don't want to. Whaddya say, babe?" I kissed her face, that part closest to her ear, where short spirals of wiry hair fell against her cheek.

Charlotte sucked her teeth. She reached back and patted my ass. "No, Patrice. Let's just get some sleep."

And having taken the final steps of our nightly waltz, I turned my back against her and forced my eyes closed.

◆

CHARLOTTE KICKED HER HEAVY boots off at the door, causing a loud thud that turned me around. Her baggy jeans were rolled into wide cuffs, exposing white tube socks that were wrinkled and moist from being stuffed inside a pair of men's hikers for ten hours. I kept waiting for her to remove those, too—it was certainly hot enough—but she walked slowly about the room with them in place, removing the wet, sticky things only after she had retrieved her black corduroy slippers.

I leaned over the counter that separated the kitchen from the living room. My eyes fell to Charlotte's feet, caught the dark blur before she quickly stuffed them into her slippers.

"Hot out, huh?" I said, my grip firm on a sauce covered wooden spoon.

I had to say something, had to snap myself out of the trance that was the brief glimpse of her bare feet.

"It was even hotter in," she said, wiping sweat from her forehead. "I was stuck on a fucking machine all day and it blew out nothing but hot air in my face all goddamn day. I swear, Patrice, I need to find a new line of work."

She said this, as she often did, but we both knew that

nothing made her happier than keeping watch over those machines. Fixing whatever needed to be fixed whenever a light flashed on, using her hands to hang and pull the thread that her counterparts then spun into socks.

But I gave to her what I knew she needed at the time. "I'm sorry, baby," were the words.

And I was sorry, sorry that she had to spend such a long time in such discomfort if nothing else. Then, turning back to the stove to stir my spaghetti sauce once more, I laid down the spoon and joined Charlotte in the living room.

I said, "Well, I have something here that might help."

Charlotte turned as I sat beside her on the sofa. She took off her cap and flung it across the room. It landed on an empty hook next to the door. Then she untied her headscarf and stuffed it in her front pocket. She picked out her tiny curls with her hands.

"What, did you win the lottery? Can we both go in to work tomorrow and holler 'fuck you' and storm out the door?" Her face had softened considerably and she reached up to put her arm around my shoulders.

"Not exactly," I said. "But I think I do have something that would make you feel a whole lot better."

Charlotte arched her eyebrow, her interest piqued.

"Oh?" she said.

I pulled the folded white envelope from the front pocket of my jeans and handed it to her. "I picked it up at the mall this afternoon," I said.

She took the envelope from my hand and shook it lightly, her eyes never leaving mine. "Hmmm, too flat and too light to be that pair of pants I've been eyeing."

"Just open it," I said, my fingers taking on a life of their own and tapping a quick rhythm against my thighs.

And Charlotte obeyed, tearing into the envelope with the excitement of a child on Christmas morning. She looked down at the pink slip of paper, eyeing it only for a moment before she twisted her lips and nodded slowly.

"A pedicure, huh?" Her words were slow and soft.

I immediately dipped into my prepared speech. "Yes, it's a pedicure, and, Charlotte, I know it's not your thing but I figured with all those hours you've been pulling at the plant lately and all that time you're spending on your feet... well, I just thought it might help you relax."

Charlotte slid the piece of paper back into the ripped envelope and laid it on the coffee table in front of us.

"Oh, I'm plenty relaxed, Patrice," she said, "and besides, it would only be a waste when I'm going to be on my feet doing the same damage the very next day. Why don't you just use it for yourself? You like that kind of stuff."

I held up a finger. "I knew you'd say that, which is why I got two. I figured it was something we could do together. That might help you, you know, get into it a little more." I reached for her hand then.

She squeezed, lifting my hand to her mouth and kissing it. "I'll never get into it. I'm just not your manicure, pedicure kind of girl. You knew that when you met me, Patrice."

"I know, I know," I said, "I guess I swung and missed, then."

"Thought that counts, dear, but I thank you for thinking of me, anyway."

Charlotte gripped both my shoulders and pulled me
to her. She pressed her lips against my neck and licked the
lobes of my ear. She kissed both my cheeks, brushed her
nose lightly across mine, then finally, thankfully, settled
onto my lips. She parted them gently with her tongue,
then pushed her way inside my mouth.

Our hands roaming aimlessly over each other's bodies, we stood, then staggered into the bedroom. Standing
at the foot of the bed, I reached forward and began peeling off her clothes, her thick flannel shirt first, then her
tank top. I loosened her heavy jeans next and pushed
them down her legs. They fell into a heap around her
ankles and Charlotte stepped out of them and kicked
them aside.

She kissed me quickly on the cheek.

"Just let me get this oil off me and I'll come out and
thank you properly, sweetie," she said before patting me
on the ass and slipping into the bathroom.

◆

THE WATER IN THE shower pounded hard, so hard
that it made my breath quicken and my pulse race. My
rejected efforts of a few moments before rushed from my
mind and were replaced by thoughts of Charlotte in the
shower, rubbing soap all over her body, letting the water
splash against her face and wet her hair.

I lay naked in the middle of our bed, waiting for her.

My knees bent and my hands tucked behind my head, I stared at the ceiling. I tapped my feet lightly against the mattress, hoping for some distraction.

I loved Charlotte, loved all of her. I loved her long legs and thin arms. I loved her toothy smile. But her feet, I loved those most of all. She never let me see them, ever, and I tried constantly, hoping that one day she would allow me into that space, that deepest part of her that she kept covered so well.

I tried while standing with her in the shower, thinking that maybe I'd distract her enough so that she would at least let me touch them with my own, but she stepped away every time, found a reason to be quick with her washing and step out, leaving me in the warm spray of water alone.

I understood she had sort of a tall woman's complex. They weren't small feet, after all, but then no one would expect them to be. Nothing about Charlotte said petite. A tall and dark woman with a small puff of unruly hair that sprang out from her scalp, her limbs were long and strong. Small feet on a woman of such massive stature would have been absurd, out of balance.

But even though she towered over me, was a foot and a half taller and thirty pounds heavier, Charlotte was generous with her body. She gladly offered me her fingers, her lips, even her ankles and knees but never, ever her feet. Those she saved for her thick socks and work boots or if her feet absolutely had to breathe, a pair of flat moccasins.

But still, I hoped and as I thought of them, what her

feet may look and feel like uncovered, my hands found their way there, way down between my legs. I rubbed the hairless rectangle that rested between my legs until it was wet and I slipped my fingers inside. I thought of Charlotte only a few feet away from me, wet and naked. I thought of what she would do to me once she was out of the shower and standing at the foot of the bed, presenting herself to me.

My eyes shut tight, I arched my back. I bit down on my bottom lip, my rigid fingers working a spasm between my legs.

Then I felt her. I opened my eyes, my hand relaxed. She crawled onto the bed, stretching her length over my petite frame.

"Surely, you could have waited for me," she whispered just past my ear as she tucked her leg between mine, lowered herself on top of me, and began to grind.

My hands fell to my sides, letting Charlotte take over. She worked my clit into a frenzy with her grinding and when I was so wet that she began sliding against me, she began at my mouth and kissed her way down.

Charlotte paused at my navel, tracing small, wet circles around it. Her chin pressed against my clit, she lingered there, applying enough pressure to bring me to the edge. Then she gave me her fingers, inserting them one by one until I had my fill.

Her tongue was next. She pulled it up and through the folds of my cunt. She pushed it forward against my clit. She found her way inside me, licking me in soft, slow strokes until my thighs began to tremble and I erupted in wet heat against her lips.

Charlotte crawled back up the bed and stretched her naked body beside mine. Breathless and spent, I reached over and touched her belly. I played with the vague layer of hair that lay against her cunt. I rested my hand on her thigh.

Then I looked down and saw that somehow, some-way, between the shower and our bed, Charlotte had managed to slip on a pair of bright pink socks.

◆

EARLY ON A WARM Saturday in August, I suggested we spend the day at the beach. I planned it all, bought a new bathing suit with a matching sarong, and fixed a picnic lunch. Charlotte wasn't a beach-loving, swimsuit kind of gal and I knew that, but if she were uncomfortable with idea, she didn't let on. She even took the liberty of pack-ing both our bags and setting them both by the door for our early morning departure. She set her blue net beach shoes on top of her pile of things.

I loaded the car while she finished getting ready, then she joined me on the passenger's side for the two-hour ride.

We pulled into an empty parking space near the pic-nic area and I popped the trunk. Charlotte opened her door and stood up, stretching her long body. Her white sundress flowed loosely around her. Her hair was pulled away from her face with a white scarf.

I began unloading our bags while she bent down and

slipped off her tennis shoes. Then she shed her socks.

"Could you hand me my beach shoes out of there?" Charlotte called to me.

"Sure," I said, moving things around in the trunk.

"You remembered to throw them in there, right, when you were loading the car?"

I was sure I heard panic creep into her voice.

"I'm sure I did," I said, pushing past bags and towels. "Let me see."

Charlotte came around to the back of the car and pushed frantically through the bags. She stepped back and pulled her fingers through her hair nervously.

"They're not here," she said. "You forgot them. I can't believe you forgot them, Patrice!"

"I'm sorry. They must have fallen off the pile when I was getting the stuff to the car. I didn't mean it, Charlotte." I held my hands out at my side and shrugged my shoulders.

It was to no avail. Charlotte seemed oblivious to anything I was saying.

"Just forget it," she said and began pulling her socks and sneakers back on.

"No," I said. "It's too hot for that. Besides, you'll ruin your shoes in that sand. Listen, the beach is right there," I said, pointing. "We can walk over barefoot. See, I'm leaving my shoes here, too." I stepped out of my flat thong sandals.

"Oh sure. You shouldn't have any problem taking off *your* shoes. You've got that pretty pink toenail polish to show off. And look, after that nice soak and massage they're all cute and soft looking."

"Well, yours could have been, too, Charlotte, if you had used the coupon I gave you. Then, I wouldn't have had to get two pedicures myself in a ten day period."

"Just forget it," Charlotte said. She snatched her bag form the trunk and threw it over her shoulder.

She began walking before I had even retrieved my own bag and by the time I closed the trunk and walked in her direction, she was already ahead of me, taking long, quick strides on the pavement. In that moment, I almost felt guilty for having purposely misplaced her beach shoes back in the farthest corner of the hall closet. After all, if she didn't want to show me her feet, who was I to force her.

I thought of all this as I jogged to catch up to her. Finally, I fell into step beside her and she slowed her stride enough for us to walk comfortably together along the beach.

"I told you I was sorry, Charlotte," I said. "Look, we don't have to stay if you don't want. I don't want you feeling uncomfortable."

I thought I saw her shoulders relax a little.

"It's all right," she breathed. She slowed then and paused long enough to reach over and take my hand.

We had walked for twenty minutes, walking close enough to the edge of the water for it to lap against our feet. We picked up oddly shaped seashells. Charlotte showed me a starfish. Then, when I thought it was safe enough to look down, I finally caught a glance at her bare feet sinking into the wet sand.

With each step, the light brown sand covered her feet, then the water crashed against them and washed it all off, exposing again the smooth dark skin underneath. Distracted by the vision, I stumbled and fell against her, causing Charlotte to lose her own footing and step sideways.

"*Fuck*!" Her scream was loud and sharp and her hands immediately left my shoulders and reached down to meet her foot, dripping from the bottom with blood.

My eyes stretched and my mouth fell open. "Charlotte, oh no!"

I saw then that a piece of broken seashell was wedged in the bottom of her foot.

Charlotte's body began to shake. Her lips trembled. I reached for her before she lost her balance, and helped her lower herself to the ground.

When I dared to look, I saw that the broken shell had left a gash in her foot that stretched from the ball to the heel and was dripping blood, dyeing the brown sand red.

I pulled my sarong from around my waist and wrapped it around her foot, creating a thick makeshift bandage.

"We've got to get you back to the car, honey, and I'm gonna take you to a hospital." I forced calmness into my voice.

Charlotte managed only to nod. She reached for me and hoisted herself up on her good foot. Then she balanced herself against my shoulder, leaning down against me as, together, we limped toward the car.

♦

"DOES IT STILL HURT a lot?" I looked up into her eyes.

Charlotte sat against a stack of pillows in an over-stuffed chair, her foot propped up on an ottoman. I sat on the floor in front of her, my feet tucked beneath me.

She cocked her head. "No, not a lot. It's a little sore still. And it itches."

I nodded. "Well, Dr. Anthony said the wrap can come off now. Are you ready?"

Charlotte twisted her mouth and shrugged, "May as well be."

"I'm so sorry, Charlotte," I said, my head hung so that my chin touched my chest. "This was all my fault. If I hadn't suggested we go to the fucking beach in that crowd and all that heat and on top of that I made you walk out there barefoot. It was just crazy of me, fucking crazy."

"It's all right," Charlotte said. Then she asked, "Patrice, could you unwrap it for me? I kinda don't want to see it just yet."

I looked up at her then. "Well, if you want me to. You sure it's okay?"

She nodded. "It's okay."

I reached for the small silver clip and carefully pulled it away, causing the top of the soft, stretchy bandage to fall free. I grabbed the end and began to slowly unravel.

"You know, the doctor also said you should be pulling regular shifts at the plant next week. That's good, right? I know this part time thing is just killing you."

I said all this while pulling and unwrapping unconsciously, sure that at any moment Charlotte would tense up and snatch her foot away, insisting she do it herself.

Then there were two layers left and I stopped, watching for her reaction.

She opened her eyes. "It's okay, Patrice, really. Take it off."

I continued to work the wrap until it loosened and fell completely away from her foot. Then I looked down.

"Well," she said, "what's the verdict."

I nodded. "It's not bad. Not bad at all. It's healing pretty nicely. The scar is really thin now, looks almost just like another line in your foot."

Charlotte leaned forward and rested her elbows on her knees. "So, what does it feel like?"

"What does it *feel* like?"

"Yeah, does it feel hard and rough, or is it flat and smooth... like my skin." She tilted her head, interested.

"You want me to touch it, then?" I looked to Charlotte for confirmation.

"Yes," Charlotte said, looking directly into my eyes, "touch it."

So I did. I lay a gentle hand on her injured foot. Then I pulled my finger lightly against the length of her healing scar.

"It feels nice, Charlotte. Not bad at all."

I looked up for her reaction and I saw that Charlotte was writhing in her seat and her eyes clenched shut. Her hands had become tight balls at her sides.

And so I continued. I rubbed the front and back of her foot alternately. I watched the expressions on her face go from calm to excited to blissful. She folded in her bottom lip, biting. Bracing with her feet against the palms of my hands, Charlotte lifted her ass slightly off the chair, then lowered herself down again.

Boldly, I brought her foot to my face, rubbing the sole against my cheek. I pressed her toe against my lips and kissed, softly, timidly.

Charlotte exhaled.

I took one beautiful toe into my mouth and sucked. She continued to squirm about in the chair. I kissed and licked the balls and curves of her foot, then covered the front of it with my mouth. I gently lapped her toes with my tongue, then slipped it between them, licking the soft webs.

From her mouth came a moan, barely audible but definitely there. From her body came jerks and grinds. She pressed her foot firmly against my mouth, gripped the arms of the chair roughly, and then Charlotte came, sharply and swiftly, her foot falling away from my mouth and onto the ottoman.

Charlotte reached down and brought my face to hers. She covered my mouth with her own. She raked her tongue across my teeth and sucked gently on mine. Then she lay her head on my shoulder, her breathing soft and steady.

I reached up and pulled the afghan off the back of the chair and covering my shoulders and her feet, I lay my head in her lap.

I touched her foot one final time, and my eyes fluttered closed.

PRACTICE MAKES PERFECT

KRISTIE HELMS

WAITING FOR THE LIGHT at Fifth Avenue and 47th Streets, Marcy turned to adjust the seams of her stockings. Heels planted firmly on the Manhattan curb, she pulled a leather glove off her right hand, leaned back at a slight angle, lifted the hem of her black wool winter coat with the back of her hand and, with the edge of one newly manicured nail, ran her finger down the length of her back thigh until she found the wayward spot just behind her knee. She gently pinched the thin silk material with the tips of her fingers, being careful to keep her nails from nicking the fabric, and tugged the seam of the right leg's stocking back toward the inside of her leg so that it perfectly curved along the line just behind her knee. Her new, calf-hugging, three-inch leather boots kept bunching that stocking around her knees.

All of the morning commuters at the corner of Fifth Avenue and 47th Street were dressed in some variation of corporate appropriate attire, as was Marcy. Black, wool winter coats wrapped around with scarves that were red or blue or even plain black. Marcy's scarf was a light pink. Just a little off from the others. Always just a little off.

Marcy was fully aware that the two men behind her had stopped their conversation recounting last night's Knick's game to stare at her seam. That seam. Marcy always made sure they saw that seam. She ran her smooth, white finger-tip back up that thin black line and traced the edge back up to just under her skirt, pausing for just a beat before letting her coat and skirt fall back into place.

Marcy adjusted the seams in her stockings the way other women flipped a length of hair out of their eyes. Walking up subway steps in the middle of a rush hour crush, she could straighten her seams with just enough subtlety that the Wall Street investor behind her saw only a flash of skin, a single black strap, and the small amount of plump thigh covered in a sheer black stocking that showed between the tops of her boots and the edge of her skirt. Practice makes perfect, and Marcy practiced this maneuver so often that it had become just another of her unconscious habits. Like tucking a loose strand of hair behind her ear or sucking on the ice cubes that remained at the bottom of her cup at the movies. Straightening her seams always made her feel a little better. More together. She was a little more settled knowing that her seams were securely in place.

The "Walk" light flashed and as Marcy's heels clicked efficiently along the crosswalk. She never turned around to see that the two men, who had witnessed her morning production, were left rooted to the curb, their Bergdorf loafers unable to take a step after what they had witnessed.

Walking to work, Marcy liked to look up at the buildings and pretend she was a tourist from Omaha. She imagined all tourists were from Omaha and she knew that they all looked up at the giant steel skyscrapers. Those concrete monuments that were draped in windows with views all the way out to New York Harbor. You could see forever from those corner offices.

Marcy knew she wouldn't be working much longer in one of those tight, low, three-walled gray-carpeted cubicles that came standard-issue with a boss standing over one of the walls. Bosses always seemed to think they were being charming and approachable when they leaned over Marcy's cubicle to inflict themselves onto her "to do" list.

Marcy wanted a corner office of her very own. She wanted her "to do" list to be her own. She took all of the night school classes at Manhattan Community College that her overworked credit cards would allow. She packed peanut butter and jelly lunches to save money for student fees. She studied thick economics books over morning coffee and she had been digging her way out of the temp pool for the last five years.

Marcy finally had a spot as an executive assistant that required proficiency in maintaining budget spreadsheets, being able to set up a letter merge for mailings, and putting up with pats on her ass from the firm's oversexed, overpaid vice presidents. Even with their Ivy League educations, they still dropped by to ask Marcy's opinion on which mergers and acquisitions would bring in the most money for the company and fatten their wallets with quarterly bonuses.

Today was the day that it would all come to an end.

Marcy had spent the past two months eyeing the one vice-president who didn't lean over her cubicle, who let her keep her own "to-do" list and who never once patted her ass. She had seen the way his eyes had widened slightly whenever she slipped off a pump and let the edge of her toe slide down her crossed leg while answering the phones outside of his office. He had actually said "thank you" when she had brought in the binders filled with full-color slides for a board meeting that he had forgotten to ask her to put together in his hurry to secure approval for a new project. After that meeting, she had quietly requested that she be an assistant only to him. He had approved it.

Evan was a gentleman, opening doors for her and allowing her to order first whenever she accompanied him on client lunches. She saw him chuckling to himself whenever she slipped back into her cubicle after a break, tugging a shopping bag filled with designer shoes she had snagged at yet another sample sale.

But today was the last day that Marcy would be answering phones for anyone—even someone as professional as Evan. This afternoon she and Evan were traveling an hour outside of the city to inspect a conference center where they were considering holding the next executive retreat. Marcy had been given the responsibility for finding the location, booking the caterer, and setting up the meeting space for the seventy-five executives to use in plotting their strategy for the coming year.

She had pursed her lips during her weekly reports with him, the first few times Evan began questioning the choices she had made for the retreat. Asking the type of food, how many people the various meeting rooms would hold, and even whether or not the company would be charged for local calls.

"Maybe you should just see if for yourself," she had finally said to him yesterday, after he had asked an endless series of questions about the conference center's copy room.

"Maybe I should. Book a car service for tomorrow after lunch. I want to see whether or not you've set this up properly."

She had fumed for exactly the half hour it had taken her to realize that this afternoon away from the office was exactly the time she needed to make her move. She had seen the way Evan's eyes lingered on the seams of her stockings and if the night classes weren't going to get her where she wanted to go, then Marcy was more than willing to use those seams to get a promotion out of her

executive assistant's position and into a new spot opening up in the marketing and event planning department,
which Evan had casually mentioned during one of their
meetings.

The fact that Evan's voice made her squirm in her
swivel chair whenever he called her into his office certainly didn't hurt. Powerful people had always been a
weak spot of Marcy's, but Evan's slender build, dark
good looks, and moody eyes made her nervously run her
hands up and down the tops of her bare arms whenever
she undressed for bed at night.

They rode in near silence to the conference center.
Each time Evan asked a perfunctory question to confirm
the directions or inquire about the number of people who
would be attending the retreat, Marcy would nervously
cross and uncross her legs to keep them from sticking
to the fake leather seats of the car service. After navigat-
ing the tollbooths at the George Washington Bridge, he
eventually stopped asking questions and Marcy eventually stopped squirming. They kept up the silence once
they reached the center, letting the site manager lead
them around each of the meeting room spaces.

When they had looked into the third type of suite
available for overnight guests, Evan abruptly turned to
their tour guide and said, "Would you mind leaving us
alone for an hour or so? We'd like to inspect the space on
our own."

Marcy pushed a strand of her hair behind her ear. Her
plan was working, but she wasn't the one leading it. She
ran a sweaty palm down the curve of her bottom and

wondered if she should have just studied harder—tried to have gotten a scholarship to someplace like NYU or Columbia instead of taking out student loans for community college.

As the door closed, the silence stretched out across the length of the room.

"Just how badly do you want that promotion?"

Marcy was too shocked to respond.

This was supposed to have gone more smoothly. More gracefully. It was supposed to have gone with Marcy asking the questions. She nervously slid a finger down her leg along one of her seams before turning around. She needed a moment to collect herself. A moment before the scent between her legs filled the room with her answer.

Opening her eyes, she turned to face him.

"How badly do you want to give it to me?"

Evan brought both of his hands up to cup her face. His lips met hers, crushing, filling her mouth with his unrelenting tongue. His hands reached under her pink sweater and cupped her breasts, twisting her nipples until they turned red through the thin silky tee she wore. She felt her knees go limp as he lifted the sweater over her head. Not letting her shrug it off her arms, he held the cashmere tight in a knotted bunch at the small of her back, trapping her arms in a vise.

This wasn't it. This wasn't the way she had planned it all.

Evan had other plans.

Too shocked to figure out a way to pull her arms free, Evan's hands wrapped around and into fists at her scalp, her dark curls screamed before she could and he forced her onto her knees at his feet. He pulled her head back so that Marcy was looking up, over the broad expanse of his suit jacket, up his Armani tie and into his eyes.

"I'm not going to give you anything that you don't deserve. There aren't any free lunches in this world. You know that as much as I do."

Evan pulled down his zipper.

"You've been asking for this for months."

Marcy's eyes watered as the grip on her scalp loosened just a bit.

"Now are you going to work for it?"

Marcy looked straight into Evan's eyes and nodded.

Her mouth filled with his cock. It took her a moment to realize what she was tasting. The dick in her mouth. The dick ramming the back of her throat, filling her airways so that she had to time her breaths through her own passion and out her nose, was pure silicone held in place with a leather harness.

The taste confirmed what she had known for some time. She had seen the slight bulges around his chest at the end of the day when the straps had loosened. She had his alumni magazine come into the office with a woman's name that he claimed was his sister's.

Marcy adjusted her mouth to take in more.

She wondered how long their understanding would last. How long until he turned on her and showed her up at some committee meeting; or stole an idea that she had whispered to him in a late-night dream and forced her back down to the temp pool to start all over again. Evan went limp and fell back on the bed.

Sprawled on the floor, staring at Evan's knees hanging over the bed, Marcy untwisted the cashmere sweater that had kept her arms trapped and tugged it off. In one quick, fluid, agile move, she stood upright. She kept her back to Evan, giving him an appetizing view of that bit of space between the tops of her leather boots and the bottom edge of her black wool skirt. She leaned backward at a practiced angle and raised the edge of her skirt slightly with the back of her right hand. She pulled up the dark edge of her stocking and with just her thumb and index finger, hooked the metal end of the garter strap that had popped off while she had been on her knees, back onto her stocking. She took the edge of her fingernail, painted in a pale ballet slipper pink, and ran it down the seam lying flat against her back thigh until she found the unruly spot. She carefully squeezed the sheer silk fabric with the tips of her fingers and drew the seam of the right leg's stocking back into place.

She heard Evan take a sharp intake of breath in the bed behind her. It was the same sound she had heard the two men standing on the corner or Fifth Avenue and 47th Street make.

Marcy smiled softly to herself before turning back to face Evan on the bed.

"Practice makes perfect."

THE PRESENTATION
M. J. WILLIAMZ

THE PRESENTATION WAS IN three hours. It was the biggest sales pitch of my career. So focused was I, as I searched my PowerPoint presentation yet again for anything that might make it less than perfect, that the ringing of my phone made me jump.

"Jerikson here," I barked.

"You work too hard, Baby."

The soft, husky voice melted me. I quickly scanned the outer office through the plate glass windows that enclosed my workspace, but I didn't see her.

"Where are you?" I asked in a more pleasant tone.

"I'm at the Paulson house."

"Is that being shown today?"

"No," she purred. "I just thought I'd come over here and hang out."

What was she doing? Our company modeled and landscaped designer pools. The Paulson house was empty at the moment. We had just finished the back-yard, preparing to show it at the annual Dream Homes fundraiser. Sharlene was one of our top sales represen-tatives; I was the vice president in charge of marketing. That we were an item was completely taboo. That we had been together for eight months was something no one knew but us.

"Why are you there then?"

"Why do you worry so much?" Her voice, low and seductive, sent chills through my body. I had never met anyone like Sharlene. Everything about her promoted her sexuality, from her provocative perfectly tailored skirt suits and spiked heels to the glossy red lipstick that accentuated her lips. It was all calculated. She wanted to be wanted. And want I did.

"You're working on that presentation, aren't you?"

"Yes. I need to nail this one, Baby."

"Mmm... I wouldn't mind you nailing me, Cris," she taunted.

I swallowed hard. How could I be so uptight about this presentation and yet so easily aroused by the merest suggestion from this woman?

"I need to focus, Shar." I tried to sound convincing.

"You were pretty focused last night, Cris. You didn't

have any time for me."

In my mind's eye, I could see her pouting, her lusciously full lower lip protruding slightly.

"I promise to have plenty of time for you tonight, Baby." And I meant that. Just the sound of her voice made me wet with anticipation. Not making love the previous night increased my need for her tenfold.

She laughed into the phone, a deep throaty sound that made my clit twitch.

"But I need some attention now." She dragged out the last word, leaving me no doubt that she intended for me to drop everything and please her.

"Baby, I can't help you right now. You know that."

"Mmm…and you know that just the sound of your voice gets me worked up. So, why don't you just talk to me for a while?"

I realized my chest was heaving. I felt like my arousal was obvious to the casual onlooker. Looking out at the office again, I wondered if my flushed face would give me away.

"I don't know if that's such a great idea."

"Why, Baby? Don't you like it when I'm worked up?"

"You know I do," I replied, torn between enjoying her arousal and the need to finish my work. It's just that…"

"That what? That the presentation you already have memorized is more important than me?"

"You know nothing's more important than you."

"Then talk to me, Cris." It was barely a whisper and I felt a drip in my boxers.

"But–"

"No buts." Everything that came out of her mouth sounded enticing. "Just talk to me. If you were here right now, tell me what you'd be doing."

My voice came out more like a croak. "Really, Baby..."

"Really what, lover? Really wet? Really hot? Oh, wait. We were talking about what you'd do to me. Not my current condition."

My breathing was heavy. I couldn't disguise my response.

"You'd like to be fucking me, wouldn't you, Cris?"

Oh my God! My crotch spasmed and my clit swelled.

"Or maybe you'd let me fuck you this time. Remember our four-month anniversary?"

How could I forget? I'd walked into the house with a dozen roses, intent on taking my girl out for dinner. Instead I'd found her naked, save for a harness and dildo. I'd never let anyone drive before. That night, I didn't say no.

I swallowed hard. "Yeah."

"That was hot, wasn't it? I found out you like to be fucked *hard*. I bet you didn't even know that about yourself, did you? But you do. If I was there, my fist would be so far in you, you'd come in two seconds."

She was right. I was drenched. I couldn't even answer her. The blood flow was all between my legs. I was incapable of conversation. My memory went back to the incredible feeling of her fist inside me after she'd drilled me with the strap-on.

"Do you want me, Cris? Do you want me to fuck you right now?"

I did. God, I wanted her right then. She was so seductive. And with my pussy that wet, the brain in my head was definitely short-circuiting. I swallowed again.

"You know how I'd start?" she continued.

I knew no response was required. I couldn't wait to hear what she had to say. I wondered. How far could she take this on the phone? How much would I be able to take?

"I'd start by putting my tongue in your ear. Mmmm. That feels good, doesn't it?" Her own breathing sounded labored, her arousal apparent in her voice. "I wonder what other orifices I might put it in. And probe. And lick. And nibble. And *bite*."

The last word was said with just enough force to make me jump.

"How wet are you, Cris? How swollen are you? What I wouldn't give to suck your swollen clit in my teeth. I can feel it there. Can you feel my teeth? I'm biting harder. The pain is exquisite, isn't it?"

I was swollen and throbbing. I could imagine the feeling of her teeth closing on me. The slight pain that induced so much pleasure. I bit my lower lip as I focused on what she was saying.

"You like that pain, don't you, Cris? Will you pinch yourself for me right now? Make yourself feel the pain?"

Admittedly, I thought about it but couldn't do it. I was at work, after all. And there were several employees milling about who didn't need to watch me touch myself. Not even for her.

"No? Too butch for that, huh? Well then, come to me

and let me bite you while the tip of my tongue flicks over your swollen tip. Mmmmm. I can taste it. I can feel how smooth and wet it is."

I was in pain. The desire had reached a fever pitch. I would have given anything to have her there. I squeezed my legs together, immediately regretting it as my thighs pinched my clitoris.

"You should come to me now, Cris. Why not? What are you gonna do? Go to the ladies' room and masturbate?" I didn't know if I could make it to the restroom.

"Can you get your fist inside yourself? Now that I'd like to see." Her voice wasn't much more than a whisper at that point, but I had the phone gripped hard against my ear. "You really didn't know it could be like this, did you? A butch chick like you. Being fucked by a femme like me. Let me give it to you, Baby. You don't let that happen often, I know. But you like it. You know you do. And I know you do. And you want it, don't you? You want it *now*, don't you? Mmmmmmmm..." I felt her breathing very hard in my ear. I knew that sound. I knew what was coming.

"Right—" She let out a high-pitched grunt that left little doubt what she was doing on the other end. My desire crept higher.

"Now," she exhaled into the phone.

We were silent for a moment.

"Do you want it, Cris? Do you want it right now? You can come to me. I'll help you."

"Wh—" My voice cracked. I cleared my throat. I could barely manage a whisper. "Where are you again? The Paulson house?"

"I wish I was between your legs."

I swallowed again. "I wish you were, too."

"So, come to me. Yes. I'm at the Paulson house. It's not far from you."

My legs were shaky as I got out of my chair. Our chief designer gave me a questioning look as I walked past his desk. I felt like the whole office had heard my conversation with Sharlene, like they all knew how wet I was and where I was going.

I said nothing until I got to the receptionist.

"You okay, boss?" she asked.

"Yeah. I'm fine." I was surprised that my voice was working then. "I'm just gonna go get a bite. I'll be back."

I chuckled at my own joke and headed out to my bike. When I sat down, the seam of my slacks rubbed against me, and my need for release grew. The ride over seemed to take forever; the vibrating motor between my legs teased me to the point of distraction. Luckily, the house was only a few blocks away.

Surprised to find the door locked, I knocked. Sharlene answered, but barely opened it. She peeked through the crack and then pulled it open for me to walk in. There she stood, completely naked. I immediately pulled her to me and kissed her. She was so soft and felt so good in my arms. I felt her hardened nipples against me and quickly brought my hands around to hold her breasts. She pulled away, took my hand, and led me to the couch.

She stood before me as I sat down. I looked her up and down, appreciating yet again her curves and the soft mocha pigment of her skin. The scent of her arousal mixed with her perfume made me lightheaded.

Lowering herself to my lap, she faced me. I could feel her warmth against me as she pressed me into the back of the couch. She immediately parted my lips and forced her tongue inside my mouth with a sense of urgency. As her tongue moved skillfully with mine, Sharlene moved up my thighs until she was rubbing herself against the fly of my Dockers. As much as I was enjoying the feeling, I was hit with the realization that I might come without her participation. I ended the kiss and she immediately stopped the rubbing. I looked at her questioningly, wondering what was next.

She kissed me again, softly, tenderly. I put my hands on her hips, pressing her into me. Slowly, I traced her outer thighs to her knees before sliding them up her inner thighs. My thumbs slowly teased her wet, silky curls. As the kiss intensified, I pressed my thumbs together, feeling them converge on her clit. She gasped and quickly pulled away.

Again my gaze probed her eyes, trying to read what she might have on her mind. My hands still rested on her thighs as she leaned forward and nibbled my neck while her hands slowly untucked my shirt. As she pulled the shirt over my head and greedily took a nipple in her mouth, I closed my eyes and reveled in the shockwaves she was sending through my body. She backed off my lap and stood, taking me with her. I had no qualms with her being in charge; I was in no condition to think.

When she leaned into me and again kissed me, I pressed her mouth hard against mine and slid my tongue inside to probe deeply as her fingers unbuttoned my slacks.

I braced myself for her touch as she unzipped my pants, but the touch did not come. Frustrated, I watched as she continued to peel them off, stopping briefly to slip my shoes off. I bent my knee to step out, but she stopped me. She knelt and peeled them the rest of the way down. As she was kneeling, she ran her tongue down my left inner thigh and back up my right. Needing her inside, I spread my legs slightly to allow her access, but she stopped before she got there.

She playfully pushed me back onto the couch and lifted my legs straight out to finish taking my pants off. When she had me naked, she sat on my knee, rubbing her swollen, wet clit against it. She was driving me crazy and she knew it. I moved my knee against her, feeling her wet heat sliding all over me. I wanted to feel her slickness with my fingers, taste it with my tongue. I didn't know how much longer I'd last. Needing relief, I tried to slide myself against her knee, but it was always just out of reach. Abruptly, she stopped and stood.

"Do you want me, Cris?" She finally spoke.

I nodded, my throat too parched to speak.

Still standing, she kissed me hard before pulling away and backing up.

"I bet you do."

She ran her hands up her thighs, parting herself for my viewing pleasure. I was breathless watching her.

"I bet you wish you could be inside of me, don't you?"

She slid her finger against her clit.

"I am *so* wet. And *so* ripe." She was breathing heavily as she slowly rubbed around her engorged clitoris. "And *so* ready to come."

I started to stand. She shook her head.

"Oh, no. You just sit tight."

She slid her hand farther between her legs and I could hear her enter herself. It was sheer torture watching her.

"Can you see, Cris?"

I shook my head slightly. I couldn't see as well as I wanted. I wanted to watch her fingers slide between those swollen lips and disappear inside her hot pussy.

She sat on the floor and leaned back against a chair that was directly across from the couch. She spread her legs and slid her finger inside.

"Can you see now? God, I want you to see. I feel so good; you wouldn't believe how wet I am. Can you see?"

I nodded. It was incredible watching her from across the room. I was mesmerized. I could clearly see how large her clit was. I wanted to suck on it. I could see her fingers coated in her juices. I wanted to be in her. But the torture of watching was exquisitely erotic.

"I want to see you, too, Cris. Spread your legs for me."

I spread them slightly.

"Come on, spread them wider. Don't worry, I'm not gonna ask you to touch yourself. But I want to see you. Lean back and spread them wide."

I did as she asked, making sure I could still see her. She repositioned herself and began to move her finger in and out, her eyes closing halfway. My hands were gripped at my side; I was willing myself not to move.

"How many fingers, Cris? One isn't enough." She was breathing heavily. "I need more. How many?" she asked urgently.

"Try three," I barely whispered.

"Only three? I don't know." Her head rocked back against the chair.

Her hips were moving against her fingers and were beginning to pick up speed. The only sounds were our breathing and the slick sound of her fingers as she fucked herself for me.

"I know what I need," she broke the silence. Her ability to speak impressed me. I barely could and I wasn't the one inside myself.

"What's that?" I managed.

She reached under the cushion of the chair and brought out a vibrator.

She turned it on and slowly rubbed it along her clit. I was amazed at her willpower. How could she not have come yet? I didn't know how much longer I'd be able not to.

She brought the vibrator to her mouth, slowly, torturously, licking around the tip before closing her full lips around it and sucking.

"Oh, God, Baby. You're killing me."

"Relax, Cris. Enjoy it," she cooed as she put the toy back between her legs. She positioned it just outside her juicy lips before arching herself slightly to slide it inside. She looked directly at me as she shoved it deep and let out a moan.

"Oh. My. God. That. Feels. So. *Good*."

She was moving it in and out, rubbing it against her clit and then sliding it in farther. I found my hips moving on the couch as I watched her. It was almost too much. I was considering going to her when she started to let out little mews and I knew she was close. I sat transfixed, aroused to the point of immobility as I watched her body tense then relax as she brought herself to a wonderful climax.

As soon as her breathing returned to normal, she smiled at me.

"Did you like that, Cris?"

I nodded.

"Do you still want me?"

"Oh, God, yes," I answered, and before I knew it, she crossed the room on her hands and knees and had her face between my legs, her teeth on my swollen clit. She was right. The pain was exquisite. With my body alive with pleasure, she had no problem sliding her fist deep inside me. My head flew back against the couch and my hips arched as she repeatedly slammed it deeper and deeper.

I gladly rode her fist, moving all over it as she kept forcing it deeper yet, all the while biting down on my clit and stroking the tender underside with her tongue. I was frantic with the need for release as I moved against her, and when she finally opened her mouth and sucked hard on me, I sailed over the edge into the most powerful orgasm I'd ever experienced.

But it didn't end there. My whole body continued

to explode as the orgasms flowed over me, one after another.

When the shaking finally subsided, I leaned back, thoroughly spent. Sharlene slowly pulled herself out of me and lay on the couch, her head on my lap, facing me.

Once my breathing returned to normal and there was blood flowing to my extremities, I began to stroke her hair. Looking down at her, I was amazed at how beautiful she was. She looked so content lying there with her eyes closed. I loved the silkiness of her hair on my legs.

When she opened her eyes and smiled at me, I was startled once again by the depth of the green in her eyes.

Still stroking her soft black hair, I asked, "What was that all about?"

"What do you mean?" Her voice was soft, like she'd just woken up.

"I mean the phone call. This. Where did all this come from?"

"Didn't you enjoy it?"

"Hell, yes!" I laughed. "It was incredible. Just a little out of the ordinary. Any reason for this?"

"How are you feeling, Baby?"

"Are you kidding? I'm like Jell-O here."

She smiled again, looking quite proud of herself.

"What?" I asked, laughing now.

"Since you're so relaxed…"

"Yes?"

"Why don't you go jump in the shower? Your suit is hanging in there."

"My suit?"

"Yes, my love, your suit. You have that presentation in an hour."

"Oh my God!" I'd completely forgotten.

"Oh, no you don't! I got you to relax and relaxed you shall stay."

Smiling down at her, I realized I'd never loved anybody more than I loved her at that moment.

"You're wonderful," I whispered.

"You'd better get ready," she whispered back.

◆

THAT AFTERNOON, I NAILED my presentation but I couldn't have done it if Sharlene hadn't nailed me first.

INSTANT REPLAY

DIANE THIBAULT

ANDREA ADJUSTED HER HAIR once again and looked at herself in the mirror. She asked herself why in the world she was fussing so much about her appearance before going out that Friday night. After all, Urvashi was just another ex-girlfriend she had agreed to meet for drinks, after a long and exhausting week at work.

They had broken up more than a year ago, after a short but intense relationship that had started with a bang and ended with a whimper. Andrea and Urvashi had both agreed that a serious relationship between them was a mere fantasy, best left unexplored, but their sexual connection had been downright fiery. Just before the separation, Urvashi seized upon the opportunity to move away for a promotion, and they had kept in touch irregularly since, mostly via e-mails and the occasional telephone call.

The lipstick tube fell into the sink, smearing the blinding white porcelain with a thick shock of dark red.

"Damn!"

Andrea picked it up and finished applying it, then took one last look at herself in the full-length mirror. Her perfume permeated the room and made her nervous all of a sudden. She adjusted the tight skirt she had pulled on at the last minute and undid another button of her silky blouse.

"God, I'm so pathetic. As if anything's going to happen. She's probably happily married with the girl of her dreams by now—without telling me, of course."

Andrea looked at her watch and realized that she was already ten minutes late. She ran out the door and walked quickly at first, then slowed down her pace, knowing that the restaurant they were meeting at was just around the corner from where she lived. As she approached, she found herself short of breath, her heart beating too fast. She stopped and leaned against the wall outside the restaurant. She closed her eyes and made herself relax. Andrea had a flashback of the first time she kissed Urvashi. She opened her eyes, aroused. She walked into the restaurant.

Inside, the atmosphere was hushed, just a few regulars eating and drinking, a couple of guys chatting at the bar at the back. Urvashi was nowhere in sight. Andrea sat at the bar and lit a cigarette.

"Good evening. How are you tonight?" the bartender said with a warm smile. Tall, dark, and handsome, all charms wasted on Andrea.

"Great. Just great. I'll have a—"

"—dirty martini," finished a breathless voice behind her.

Andrea turned to face Urvashi and felt herself blush. She laughed.

"Hey, gorgeous. I guess some things don't change, n'est-ce pas?" said Urvashi. She smiled and kissed Andrea on the cheek. Urvashi looked radiant with her short lustrous hair and her feminine yet slickly professional suit. What a beauty.

"No, I guess not. You still remember my tastes."

"Well, some of them, anyway," winked Urvashi.

Urvashi fixed her gaze on the bartender for a few seconds. "I'll have a classic."

She turned her attention to Andrea. "So, what have you been up to? I haven't heard from you in ages. Are you avoiding me?"

Andrea shrugged at Urvashi's legendary directness. She had never been one to keep her cards close to her chest. Andrea remembered the day Urvashi had sat her down to discuss ending their relationship. Tough love, but with a lot of tenderness underneath.

Andrea flicked her cigarette into the ashtray before taking another drag. "Well, you know...I've been busy and...I mean, I thought it would be a good idea to take some space apart. You know?"

Urvashi nodded. "Sure. Sure." She took a sip of her drink and looked around. Turning to face Andrea, she brushed her hand lightly on Andrea's skirt, arousing her further. Andrea's skin tingled at her touch.

"Don't you want to know what I've been up to?"

"Of course, Urvashi. I imagine you've been dating up a storm. Do you have a girlfriend and a white picket fence?"

Urvashi laughed. "No, silly girl, I don't." She gazed deep into Andrea's eyes, with a serious look on her face. "I haven't found anyone as wonderful as you, my dear."

Andrea lowered her eyes, shrugged, and finished her cocktail in one gulp. The restaurant was filling up and the conversations ebbed and flowed in keeping with a soft mid-tempo jazz set in the background.

"Would you like another?" asked the bartender.

"Absolutely," said Andrea, surprised at her own foolishness. She felt as though she were walking into a spider web, and being willingly led into it.

Urvashi looked away, then at her. "Listen. I didn't ask to meet you so we could, you know, get back together. I know we're not meant to be in a relationship together. But I just...I'm so attracted to you and well...I think you feel the same way, no?"

"Urvashi–"

"Look...I just want to follow you home tonight. I want to make love with you. It used to be so good, remember?"

Andrea paused to light another cigarette and contemplate the murky waters of her martini. She remembered all too well. Meeting Urvashi at an art show and engaging her in a conversation. Going out for a cigarette. Urvashi following her into a corner on the side of the building, away from the crowd. Andrea saying a few sweet words, then kissing Urvashi on impulse, and being pleasantly surprised at her reaction, as she pushed Andrea against a wall and worked her hands up her blouse and under her bra with the skill of a seasoned expert. Not here, not now, whispered Andrea. Both of them going back to Andrea's place and almost tearing each other's clothes off. Making love all night, taking turns, talking dirty, then falling asleep, exhausted, like wild animals after a successful hunt followed by a plentiful feast. In the morning, they had sex again a few times, unable to satisfy their thirst for each other, then finally, laughing, admitted to a more mundane type of hunger and went out for brunch. The first of several dates, heated and passionate, before the inevitable parting.

Urvashi quietly sipped her martini and observed Andrea.

"So...is this what you want? Go back to my place and fuck? No promises? No strings attached?" said Andrea.

"Well...yes. Yes, I do."

"Then finish your drink, because I think we might have to skip dinner."

Andrea smiled, and Urvashi grinned. She gulped down the rest of her martini and put her credit card on the counter, pushing Andrea's hand away with a swift gesture.

"No, gorgeous, it's on me." Sweet words. Promising and scary at the time.

As they walked back to Andrea's place, Urvashi told her more about her recent life.

"So, after the promotion, the boss sent me around the world. I thought it'd be fun to travel everywhere, but mostly I was just exhausted and I barely saw anything in all the great cities I visited. Finally, I applied for another position, one that only involves occasional trips, but is mostly based in the city. I've been dating around, had a few flings, but that's it. What about you?"

Andrea thought about how much she should reveal. But she felt heady with alcohol and decided not to hold back, for once in her life.

"Well...I did date somebody for a while, a few months after you left. I mean, after we broke up. Cute young thing, totally wrong for me."

"Oh, one of those–" Andrea thought that she would catch Urvashi smiling, but she was dead serious. She looked as though she was recalling something which she didn't wish to share.

Andrea walked on, then, felt Urvashi grabbing her hand. The warmth of Urvashi's hand stirred Andrea and made her want to make love with her right now, any- where, in any corner they could have found. They were almost at the door of her apartment.

"Andrea."

Andrea turned around while fishing for her keys in her purse. Urvashi smiled and nodded for her to open the door. Andrea unlocked it, then entered her apart- ment with a shiver.

"Do you want a drink or–" Andrea started, but before

she could continue, she felt Urvashi grab her waist from behind.

"I want you."

Urvashi turned her around and pushed her against the wall.

"Oh, baby." A groan escaped Andrea's lips.

Urvashi caressed her neck with her lips, teasing Andrea like she used to, but without granting her the deep, passionate kiss she knew she craved. Urvashi pressed her body against Andrea's, not letting her move an inch.

"I know what you want, baby."

"Do you?" Andrea challenged her, looking directly into her eyes.

"I know what you need." Andrea felt her heart leap at the thought of how Urvashi used to take her sexually, and how much she loved every second of their encounters.

"Let's go into your bedroom." Andrea walked obediently into her bedroom, with Urvashi following her closely behind.

"Close your eyes, Andrea." The whisper of Urvashi's sensuous voice melted all of Andrea's doubts about having sex with her again. She felt completely at her mercy, a delicious sensation. She smiled.

Urvashi made Andrea sit on the bed, then approached her and grabbed her hair, pulling lightly. A moan escaped out of Andrea's mouth.

"Oh, please."

"Really? Is this what you want? Are you still a bad, bad girl? Are you?"

"Yes," Andrea pleaded. "Yes, I am. I'm your bad girl. I'm your slut." She surprised herself with the rawness of her desire, as Urvashi continued to pull her hair, and started to run her other hand down her cleavage.

With a swift hand, Urvashi undressed Andrea down to her underwear. She was wearing a lacy red bra and a thong. Urvashi's mouth watered at the thought of tasting her. She slipped her hand between Andrea's legs.

"What's this? Are you wet? Have you been wet all evening?"

Andrea blushed and giggled, her arousal running like wildfire through her body. She remembered Urvashi's hands, all over her, deep inside her, and still wanting more. Urvashi's fingers slipped briefly inside her. She screamed.

"Careful, the neighbors might hear you. Remember?" Urvashi laughed gently at the memory. It was so easy to tease and humiliate Andrea, a slave to her own desires and her body's restless demands.

"Andrea."

"Yes?"

"Lie down." As if in a dream, Andrea obeyed her and lay down on her large bed, cushioned by luxuriously fluffy pillows, feeling as though she were lost on a raging sea with nothing to hold on to.

"Close your eyes."

Almost immediately, she felt Urvashi tie something soft but strong on her head to blindfold her, and something made of the same material around her wrists. Had Urvashi planned all this in advance? It only took her two or three minutes to tie her down, and then Andrea was her prisoner.

"Remember, Andrea? Remember how good it felt to fuck all night, and all day? Remember when I used to take you and you let me in, each and every time?"

Andrea's mind was buzzing and she pondered whether or not she should respond out loud to Urvashi's teasing reminiscences of their sexual involvement, when she felt her legs being parted.

A silky tongue soon started licking her clit, and Andrea thought she would not be able to control her moans, though she tried her best. Urvashi slipped a couple fingers in, then a couple more.

"Oh, god, Urvashi...oh, you're not...? Are you...? I don't know if I can stand it."

"Yes, you can. Come on, baby, let me in. You know how good this feels. Let me give it to you."

Urvashi gradually entered her more deeply and soon, her entire fist was moving gently inside Andrea's cunt, who felt herself rushing toward an explosive orgasm, her legs trembling, before she let go and came with a series of uncontrollable moans.

"That's right. That's right, Andrea. That's a good girl. That's my good girl."

After Andrea was spent and unable to struggle with her bonds, Urvashi came up to her and undid her blindfold. Andrea's eyes were brimming with tears, not quite ready to fall, and Urvashi smiled with her.

Urvashi kissed Andrea at last, a long, deep, slow and sensual kiss that sent shivers up Andrea's spine. She was by far the best kisser Andrea had ever dated.

Urvashi untied her and pulled her close. They held on to each other quietly, then Andrea came out of her glow.

"Urvashi...you are so great. You are such a great lover, I mean. Let me–"

Andrea started caressing Urvashi, paying attention to her breasts, and pulling on her nipples, which clearly delighted her, though Urvashi was quieter than Andrea, though no less passionate.

"Wait," Urvashi interrupted.

"What?" Andrea said quizzically.

"Only if I can stay overnight. I've got a lunch tomorrow, but...I'm free until then."

Urvashi stared at Andrea, waiting for a response, unsure.

"Yes, of course. I wanna fuck you as long as I can."

Urvashi replied by opening her body to Andrea.

CRUISING

RASHELLE BROWN

VALERIE'S VACATION HAD SLIPPED away in stages. The first day and a half, she had simply been overwhelmed: The food, the parties, the nearly 2,000 women dressed in everything from thong bikinis to saris—all packed onto a ship bound for the heart of the Caribbean. The sheer liberation of it all had rendered her unable to act. She merely floated along with the tide, head buzzing, eyes popping, mouth perpetually turned upward in a stupefied grin.

By the end of day two, though, she was used to it all, and she needed to act. She was aware of the passing of each hour, and she began to form plans for fulfilling her mission: to find a woman of her own among the common throng.

Day three involved a long shore excursion on Half Moon Cay that yielded nothing. At dinner that night, her time was monopolized by a rather drunk couple who seemed to be looking for a third—not something she was interested in.

The fourth day had shown some promise—she'd had a nice, flirty conversation with a very attractive woman at one of the pools. They'd made plans to meet for a drink before dinner and maybe catch the evening show together. But the woman never showed up at the bar. Valerie looked for her in vain at dinner. She spotted her later, at the show, with a much younger woman. Valerie skipped the show and went back to her cabin. Depression had set in.

Day five was what she considered her "lost" day, the one she wished she could get back. She spent the morning ashore, wandering among the tourist-trap huts located within a half mile of the pier, feeling alone and sorry for herself. In a move of desperation, she signed up for the Singles Speed Dating event that was to take place at 4:00 P.M. in the main ballroom. She spent the whole afternoon worrying about it and changing her mind about whether she would actually go or not. At 3:00 P.M., she decided that she would definitely not go. At 3:30 P.M., she was seized with panic—leaving this ship without even one date would drive her self-image into the abyss. She had to go. She ran to her cabin, showered in ten minutes, then tried on every piece of clothing she'd brought on the boat. Sweating and near tears, she left her cabin at 3:55 P.M. wearing the same outfit she'd worn ashore that morning—she liked the way the shirt clung to her breasts.

Arriving at the ballroom only two minutes late, she was greeted by a sturdy woman who handed her a name tag and a magic marker. "Welcome to Singles Speed Dating! Write your name on the tag and place it prominently about your person," she chuckled. "You don't have to use your real name!" Valerie wanted to turn and run. Later, she would wish with all her heart that she had, but she didn't. Instead, she wrote "Valerie" on her name tag and stuck it to her clingy top, just above her right breast.

What followed were the two longest hours of Valerie's life, broken into five-minute segments, each one more ludicrous than the last. Women had names like "Barbie" and "Penelope" written on their name tags. They were big, small, loud, shy, dykey, femme, and not one of them piqued her interest or her libido at all. She blamed it mostly on her own attitude—there were attractive women there; she just assumed that something must be wrong with them if they were here doing this. Something was wrong with her, after all, wasn't it? Wasn't she too shy, or too boring or too constrained? Isn't that why women looked past her or through her and ended up with a younger, more "alive" prospect at the end of the night?

Feeling worse than ever, Valerie trudged back to her cabin in a daze. Just as she reached her door, a group of women passed by, laughing and talking. The woman at the tailend of the group looked at Valerie. Her eyes fell immediately to Valerie's chest. She smiled. Valerie felt elated for a moment, but then remembered that she was still wearing her name tag. Had that been a smile of pity? Her foul mood assumed that it was. She went inside her cabin, plopped down on the bed, and ordered room service. She wouldn't be going out again.

And so, here it was, the last night of her seven-day cruise. Wanting to take *something* positive back with her, Valerie vowed that she would enjoy this last night. She would not waste it looking for something. Rather, she would enjoy what was all around her: the sea air, the four-star cuisine, the rooms and pools and decks full of women.

She dressed for dinner in the formal gown she had splurged on two months ago, when this trip was all mystery and anticipation. It *was* a great dress, and she looked great in it. It hugged and flowed in just the right spots to make her seem five—maybe ten—years younger. She took her time getting ready, sitting in front of the mirror, the way she imagined the rich must do every day. It was fun. Yes, this was more of what she needed—the here and now—and less of tomorrow and yesterday.

Throughout dinner Valerie tasted each bite of food, inhaled deeply the aroma of each sip of wine, and feasted her eyes on the women around her. She appreciated each one of them without asking herself, "Is she single? Is she looking at me?"

After dinner, she went down to the pool deck where

the brassy glint of the late evening sun caressed only a handful of shoulders. Across the pool, near the bar, a woman was standing alone with a glass of wine in one hand, shielding her eyes from the setting sun with the other. She looked so serene.

That's how I want to be, Valerie was thinking, *content*, and then the woman turned her head and looked at Valerie.

Valerie held the woman's long gaze and smiled. The woman turned toward her then, lowering the hand from her eyes. Then she took a step in her direction, and Valerie bit the corner of her mouth, turning her smile into a twisted grin.

Another step and another—yes, the woman was walking toward her. The small bit of contentment Valerie had been feeling evaporated. It morphed into nervousness, then doubt, then ebbed into curiosity.

With each step the woman took across the deck, Valerie became more intrigued. She possessed an ageless quality, a kind of visual lesson in subtle contradictions. From a distance it could be seen in the way she carried herself: she exuded a graceful self-confidence—completely lacking bravado—that belied one of the sexiest bodies on the ship. As she drew nearer, the setting sun glinted off a few gray hairs nestled in among thick, brown satin. Finally, standing face to face with her, Valerie saw fine lines at the corners of her eyes and mouth that blended smoothly into the most flawless skin she had ever seen. When the woman smiled at her, something in Valerie was set in motion. A switch had been thrown;

there was current moving through her.

"Hi. I'm Pandora," the woman said.

"*Pandora*," Valerie repeated it, creasing her brow. It was so wrong.

"No, not really," the woman laughed. Her smile was debilitating. Valerie stood in wonderment, unable to even smile back. The woman continued quickly, "It's Joan. That's so boring, though, I thought I'd spice it up."

"No, it's not," Valerie managed. "Not boring. I love that name. Like Joan of Arc." She sounded like an idiot. She *wasn't* an idiot, though. She had to do something, *say* something that made her not sound like a social imbecile. "Would you like to get a drink?" she blurted.

Joan laughed, raising her wine glass. "I've already got one. Let's go get you one, though."

Valerie's head was whirling. This woman seemed interested in her—had crossed the deck of this ship for her. She took a deep breath, mustered a smile, and headed for the bar.

"What'll you have, ladies," the bartender asked.

"Gin and tonic, please," Valerie said.

"I'm good," Joan said. She winked at Valerie.

"Do you want to watch the sunset?" Valerie asked, feeling a little more confident.

"That's exactly what I want to do," Joan said.

Out on the promenade deck and halfway through her G&T, Valerie felt as high as she had ever been. She had relaxed completely and the conversation was flowing like honey. She felt so at ease with Joan, yet every few minutes a voice in the back of her head would shout, "I can't believe this is happening!" Then she would smile and try to make it work with the conversation. Joan caught her once and asked, "What? Did I say something funny?"

"No," Valerie said. "I'm just happy."

Joan nodded and smiled back. "I know what you mean." She touched Valerie's bare shoulder and ran a finger down her arm, then onto her hip and around the small of her back. She set her drink on the deck rail and moved directly behind Valerie. She put her hands on Valerie's hips and pulled her close. The first stars began to show in the sky.

Valerie leaned back a little, feeling Joan's breasts against her back. Joan moved her hands around Valerie's waist. She pressed against her with her whole body. "God, you smell good," Joan whispered.

Valerie glanced quickly from side to side. There were other couples, spaced at intervals, doing exactly what they were doing. This emboldened her.

Electric current popping in her veins now, she placed a hand lightly atop one of Joan's and pressed gently downward. Joan took the cue. She kissed the side of Valerie's neck and moved her hand farther down. She hovered there for a moment, her lips parted slightly on Valerie's neck. Then she moved her fingertips and her tongue in unison.

Valerie gasped, grabbing the deck rail. Joan's tongue moved in soft whorls against her neck, the touch of her fingertips was just perceptible. The combination of the two sensations summoned the animalistic part of Valerie's brain. She had lost herself completely. She no longer cared where she was or who was there. "Oh, *God*," she whispered.

Joan responded with the slightest increase in motion. Direction and rhythm now emerged. Her lips softly withdrew from Valerie's neck and moved to her ear. "I want to take you here," she whispered. "Right now."

Valerie's eyes lifted open. It was almost full dark. Soft arcs of yellow light fanned out at intervals up and down the deck, but they, like the other couples, were standing in a dark space between the lamps. She could just make out the silhouettes of the next couple down the row. "Yes," she whispered.

Joan moved immediately. She reached her hands down and lifted the sides of Valerie's dress just enough to get some play in the fabric. Then she hooked her thumbs into the waistband of Valerie's panties and pulled them down to mid-thigh level, returning the dress to its proper place all in one motion. She moved her hand back around to the inside of Joan's thigh and the sensation was explosive.

Valerie pulsed and hardened at Joan's touch, and in the next instant she felt the wet against the smooth rayon of her dress.

"I've been watching you, imagining this for two days," Joan said.

Valerie only moaned in reply. She widened her stance a little, her panties stretched taut around her thighs. Here was the unbearable time—that string of moments that oscillated violently between needing to come so badly and wanting this to last forever.

Joan began slowly reeling Valerie's dress up by handfuls. The removal of her hand brought Valerie into raging consciousness. Stars glared down on them. There was no moon yet. The lamplights seemed to shine more dimly and from farther away.

"I need it *now*," Valerie said, voice faltering. She had never been so exposed. She had never cared so little.

"I know you do," Joan smiled, gathering up the final handful of rayon. She moved one of Valerie's feet in with her own foot, then stripped Valerie's panties to the deck floor with it. She turned Valerie around gracefully and crouched in front of her.

"Oh, no—" Valerie started a protest, but then Joan's mouth was on her and she could not speak.

Valerie leaned back hard against the deck rail, grabbing it with both hands. She tensed for a moment, hearing voices emerge from the dining area out onto the deck, but then it was too late—she had entered the gauzy tunnel that distorted her senses, and soon nothing existed except for her and Joan and the solid wood of the deck rail.

She could feel it coming fast. She rose up onto her toes and Joan took this as an invitation to enter her. Valerie moaned loudly and threw her head back. All at once full sensation returned, and she was aware of the cool night breeze, the scent of the sea, the light of the moon that had just cleared the horizon. She took it all in, and one sensation more: the cool, smooth skin of Joan's face against her taut thighs. Here was a woman—*this beautiful woman*—making Valerie feel like she had never felt before.

"Yes!" she shouted, quivering on tiptoe. Joan moved a

hand up to the small of Valerie's back and pulled, holding Valerie tightly there against her mouth. "Oh, God, yes!" Valerie bellowed again. A smattering of applause and laughter could be heard up and down the deck.

Joan looked up at her out of breath. "Was it good?" she asked

Valerie stared down at her in disbelief. "I...don't...*do* things like this."

"Neither do I," Joan smiled. "I mean, not right out in the open like this. Would you like to come to my cabin?"

Valerie stepped back, feeling dizzy. She drew in a hefty portion of the warm sea air. She paused, savoring the moment for a long while, and only one thought repeated itself in her head.

"You mean we could've been doing this for two days?"

THE TAPPING OF KEYS

EVA HORE

CAREFULLY TRYING TO AVOID potholes, I idled slowly up the long winding driveway. It was a kilometer from the turnoff and I was nearly there. Small branches and leaves covered the ground and more than once the car fishtailed, almost connecting with trees that haphazardly paved the way.

I breathed a sigh of relief when I finally made it to the cabin in one piece. I hadn't been up here for ages. Opening the car door my senses were assaulted with the heady fragrance of eucalyptus gums and rich composted earth. There was the faint hint of rain, tantalizingly fresh, lingering on the cool autumn air.

Anticipating a storm could be brewing, I hurriedly unpacked the boot and dumped my luggage on the front porch. With leaves crushing beneath my feet I skirted around the cabin to the old water tank, fiddling beneath until my fingers located the keys. I shuddered at the thought of a hairy spider running over my hand and was pleased not to have encountered any.

I stopped at the long-standing barn; fond memories flooding back as I looked beyond the rise, to see the sparkle of running water from the creek that ran through our property.

Yanking open the door, I made the rusty hinges groan in protest. I checked on firewood that was stacked high, pleased to see there was ample. My fingers ran across the ancient mud brick and splintered wood of one of the stalls. How many stories did this barn hold? I chuckled, remembering that it was here that I had my first sexual experience.

That was so long ago.

Hurrying back, my arms brimming with dried out logs, I tripped over a loose stone, dropping a few as I righted myself. It reminded me just how careful one had to be up here. There were no phones and reception for my mobile was usually nonexistent.

My nose wrinkled; dust and the distinct unpleasant odor of mice hung in the air as the front door to the cabin creaked open. I threw open all the windows and back door to give the cabin a good airing while I dusted and made up my bed. Within the hour the house was fresh and presentable.

Flicking on the switch for the hot water service, I set about lighting a fire in the hearth. As it crackled to life I hurried outside to replenish the now empty wood box. Loaded down with red-gum logs, I heard the first boom of thunder echoing in the valley below.

The screeching of cockatoos and the laughter of a kookaburra had me searching the sky for them. They were hidden, somewhere amongst the spindly trees, deep in the forest.

At the front door I turned and watched the sun begin to slip away. It had been mostly hidden by rolling, rumbling clouds, its redness desperately breaking through to give the forest a stained pink hue. It was still early, but here in the forest the afternoon quickly turned to dusk. Just then huge splats of rain hit the old tin roof; the fragrance of the forest rose to tantalize my nostrils as it combined with the wonderful smoky aroma coming from the chimney.

Locking all the windows and doors, I placed a bottle of wine in the freezer and a lasagna to heat in the oven while I ran the bath. I lit candles, giving the room a seductive feel and then slipped into the old bath, immersing myself in soap and fragrant bombs.

With my head resting comfortably on the rim of the bath I cleared all negative thoughts and looked forward to these three days, three days of no interruptions and the ability to conclude the final chapter of my novel.

I'd been working on my novel for over a year and was eager to finalize it. The last chapter needed my uninterrupted attention. I had a sex scene to work on and was uncomfortable at having to delve into my subconscious, part of me not wanting to remember how wonderful it all had been. It had been over five years since I'd had sex, five years since Mary had died. I hoped my sadness would not continue to hinder my writing.

I watched the soapy suds rise and fall over my breasts as my breathing quickened. I was remembering a time when Mary and I had come here for a naughty weekend, a time when all the inhibitions I had went out the window.

Running my hands over my breasts I closed my eyes and imagined Mary was with me now, that it was her hands caressing me, her fingers that were tweaking my nipples and now her hand that was inching its way down to my mound before it disappeared between my thighs.

My eyes were still closed. The hand on my breast tugged harder at the nipple, drawing it out, squeezing it between my fingers while the other slipped over my slit before parting the folds and gently sliding its way in.

Pulling the hood back over my clit, I began to rub in small circular motions, enjoying the sensation as the nub hardened under my fingertips. The water felt delicious, gliding as though caressing my body. I opened my legs wider, experiencing that desperate urge to come, the urge I hadn't been able to bring to fruition all these years.

I rubbed harder, zoning in on the exact spot. My eyes were still closed, all thoughts of Mary now prominent in my mind. Her beautiful face swam before me, her pouting lips whispering what I longed to hear. I was nearly there, nearly peaking. Concentrate I told myself. I desperately needed to come.

A branch fell across the tin roof, startling me. My eyes flew open, my vulnerability paramount in my mind as I lay naked in the bath. I held my breath then breathed a sigh of relief when I heard a squirrel scampering across the roof.

My mood broken, I rose, catching a glimpse of my naked body as I stepped out of the bath and faced the full-length mirror. Chilled by the cool air, my nipples became rigid, and just before I enveloped myself in a large bath sheet I watched the soapy suds fall from me to disappear into the foam backed mat.

I hurried to the fire, opening the towel to bare myself, the goosebumps disappearing as the heat spread over me. I picked up the old flannelette nightie I'd placed to warm on the chair and slipped my feet into furry slippers.

A quick brush of my hair, and my long curly locks were tied up in a hair clamp. Wrapping a woolen robe around me, I hung the towel over the chair to dry and made my way into the kitchen.

The lasagna was perfect and the bottle of wine just what I needed to warm up my insides. When I finished, I placed the dirty dishes in the sink and carried the wine and my glass over to the desk.

Lifting the cover of my old Olivetti typewriter, I sneezed as dust particles flittered about the air. From the drawer I withdrew some paper, a bottle of white out, just in case of mistakes, and rolled the first sheet in. It took me a few minutes to get into the chapter and the next thing I knew my fingers were tapping away madly.

With the rain pelting down on the roof and my fingers flying over the old keys, I set about to construct and explore a sexual encounter to stop my readers in their tracks. Downing the wine, I lost myself in a world that only fellow writers can understand.

Three hours later and the empty bottle of wine long gone, I'd finished my first draft, pleased with how it had gone. I threw more logs onto the fire, removing my dressing gown as I hurried into the kitchen to uncork a fresh bottle.

Rummaging around in the fridge, I opened up the cheese and fruit containers. Arranging the food on a platter, I took it and the wine back into the cozy lounge to sit comfortably on the couch and relax. I went over the scene I'd written in my head, wondering if I'd been explicit enough or if tomorrow I'd find the chapter useless.

It bothered me that I wasn't comfortable writing sex scenes; all good writers should be. It was no different than writing about a murder, or a comedy. They were just words, words put into a specific order to titillate and arouse the reader.

My eyelids grew heavy, the wine making me sleepy, and before long I pulled up a rug and settled back on the couch to have a short nap. I thought of Mary as the rain, now torrential, slammed down on the roof, the noise deafening, yet comforting as it lulled me to sleep.

I slept longer than planned and woke to see that everything outside had turned pitch black, just the occasional flash of lightening searing the sky as it sparked angrily in the storm.

Looking at my watch, I was surprised it was already nine o'clock. I made myself a strong coffee, grabbed a biscuit, and sat back at the typewriter to read back what I'd written. What I read shocked me. I hadn't typed these words, cock, pussy, fuck, and cunt. Where had they come from?

Ripping the paper from the rollers I crinkled it up and threw it into the fire. My hands shook as I surveyed the room. I knew everything was locked and surely I would have known if someone had come in, so how on earth had I managed to write such filth.

I typed, *Final Chapter*, on the clean sheet of paper. Staring at it, I was at a loss for the words to begin. The coffee began to clear my head but I was left with an uneasy feeling. A feeling of being watched. Words like murder, tortured, hacked and such, raced through my mind.

Closing the curtains tightly, I rechecked the doors and poured myself some cognac. Downing the drink quickly, I listened for anything out of the ordinary. Nothing. Apart from the steady beat of the rain, the occasional clap of thunder, nothing else was amiss.

I picked at the cheese, swallowed a strawberry, a piece of mango, and filled up my glass again. I was nervous and slightly afraid. With the fire still blazing I snuggled up on the couch, my head cradled on my arm as I watched the flames flicker and grow. Before long my eyelids became heavy once more.

Suddenly something was on me. My eyes flew open;

my heart pounding madly, the empty glass falling to the floor as I grappled with, with…nothing. Nothing was there. Yet something seemed to be lying on me. A weight had descended upon me. I could see nothing but feel it all.

I was terrified and alarmed, especially when I saw my nightie being inched up my leg, over my thigh, my stomach, and up higher to completely expose my breasts. I froze as something tugged at my arms, my nightie being pulled over my head only to be discarded on the floor. I lay there breathing hard, naked on the couch.

I tried to cover myself but hands, unseen hands, pulled my arms up over my head. My breasts jutted forward, hardening as something cold sucked one into what could have only been a mouth. The keys on the typewriter began to tap.

Tap, tap. Words, lots of words made their way on the paper.

I opened my mouth to scream and something covered it, a cold tongue snaked in and thrust itself down my throat. I struggled against this…this being. I tried to buck it from me, but I could not. It was too strong and pinned me down easily.

Tap, tap, more words.

My legs were yanked apart and cold fingers were pulling at my pussy lips, tugging at them, fiddling with my clit, driving me wild. A cold finger entered me, fucking me deliciously while still rubbing my clit.

My breasts were squashed, nipples nipped at, teased and then swallowed. A cold tongue circling them, causing them to stand rigid while my pussy was still being fingered, fingered carnally, but now I was no longer frightened, I was loving it, wanting it, desperate for more.

I closed my eyes; allowed myself to relax, to enjoy whatever it was that was happening to me. Hands ran over my body, touching, feeling, and exploring while a mouth kissed me, kissed me passionately.

Tap, tap, more and more words.

Then I was carried, or levitated, whatever you please, and placed on the floor, on the old cowhide. My arms and legs spread-eagled, hands on my wrists and ankles holding me down. It was frighteningly erotic and I was wild for it, for all of it.

A mouth was back on my pussy, but this mouth was different, this mouth was soft and demanding, touching me like only another woman would know. I wished I could see who this was. What this person looked like. Instead I could only fantasize and I conjured up a gorgeous looking woman with huge breasts, a luscious pussy, a pussy that I could kiss, lick, touch, and taste. A woman like Mary.

A cold nipple was thrust into my mouth and I sucked on it, sucked it hard into my mouth, enjoying the feel of it as it grew. I could feel cold fingers on my pussy lips, opening them and then sliding right in, spearing me, digging into my insides to rub at those delicious areas, to find my G-spot and make me come.

Tap, tap, tap, more and more words.

My ankles were released and I left them open for my unseen lover, urging her on, wanting her to continue, to continue finger-fucking me like I've never been fucked before.

I was suffocating from the breast in my mouth that also covered my nose, the weight of it smothering me. I was wild as other hands fondled my breasts, pinched my nipples, sucked and licked while the fingers continued to fuck my pussy.

I was moaning, trying to scream out. I pushed the breast away from my mouth so wild with passion that I had to tell them, tell them all how I felt.

"Fuck me! Fuck me with my dildo. It's in my bag. Fuck me harder, harder," I begged, screaming into the quiet cabin. "Fuck me you bitches, whoever you are."

And when they found my dildo, they did, over and over, until one of them grabbed me, rolled me over onto the hide, and pulled me up by the hips so I was in the doggy position. Now I was being slammed into; my hair having fallen from its clasp was a tangled mess, covering my face as she thrust that dildo into me.

My tits were jiggling all over the place, hands were trying to grab hold of them, but the force of the dildo fucking had me burning my knees on the hide as whoever it was, pummeled into me.

Tap, tap, more and more words written on the white pages, the ink leaving its mark.

"Fuck me harder," I screamed again. "I'm coming, I'm coming."

And I did. I came and came. This unseen lover would not stop and just as I'd finish one orgasm another would take over my body, until I thought I'd pass out. Finally she stopped, pulling away from me and I fell facedown onto the floor, my breasts squashed beneath me, my breathing ragged as I tried to pull myself together.

And still the keys continued to tap.

"Who are you?" I asked.

No answer except for the tapping of the keys.

I made to get up but I was pulled back down again. I lunged for my handbag. I'd left it beside the couch. Opening the latch, I pulled out my clit vibrator, I never left home without it.

Something snatched it from my hand as I watched mesmerized as it made its way down toward my pussy. I turned my head and saw that somehow they'd discovered my strap-on dildo, the dildo that I'd left here after Mary had died.

I couldn't stand to throw it away, and I couldn't leave it at home. Seeing it brought up magical memories, memories of our love for each other and how fantastic our sex life had been before she'd died. I had no more time to think about it as once again I was pulled up to a standing position, my legs weak and shaky.

The strap-on dildo made its way down toward the cowhide and I lunged for it, wanting to do as I pleased but was held back by cold hands. The dildo was standing up from the floor and hands now released me so I could straddle the realistic shaft. I held onto the couch as I lowered myself over the knob. I watched in awe as it parted my lips and slipped inside me, my pussy lips opening wider, kissing its girth as I stretched to accommodate it.

Tap, tap...tap, tap. I fleetingly wondered just exactly

what the words were what they were typing.

Slamming myself down on the dildo, I ground myself into it, loving it and what it was doing to me. My breasts jutted forward and someone tweaked the nipples as the clit vibrator buzzed crazily over my clit.

"Oh yeah. That's fucking great," I screamed as another orgasm ripped through me. "Oh yeah, fuck me, fuck me you cunts."

Now something was pushing me from behind, pushing me to bend over. My tits swayed and I watched mesmerized as the unseen mouth sucked a nipple in. I could see the skin stretch, the nipple being pulled forward, and all my senses went crazy as I felt something probe my arse.

I've never been fucked up the arse and I tried to look over my shoulder, to see something but all I could see were my cheeks being pulled apart and I lay forward, eagerly anticipating my first arse fucking.

Slowly the dildo inched its way in. My hips were being held firmly as she pushed in slowly, while the woman beneath me began to thrust the strap-on upward. Soon both the dildo and vibrator were fucking like crazy and I didn't know which one was giving me the most pleasure.

It was fucking amazing.

I was screaming, throwing myself around like a mad woman. Never in my life could I have possibly imagined anything like this. Even as a writer there was no way my imagination could have possibly been stretched that far.

"Fuck! Oh fuck yeah, harder! Harder! You fucking

bitches," I screamed as another orgasm gushed from me.

My body was weak from all the lovemaking. My legs began to shake as they gave it their all. The one fucking my arse finally collapsed on my back while the one beneath me slowly stopped.

Then they lifted me gently and placed me on the couch, covering me with a rug. I was breathing slowly, the tapping of the typewriter keys was winding down, and then as my eyelids grew even heavier they stopped all together. Totally and deliciously fucked I fell into a deep sleep.

I woke in the morning battered and bruised. It took me a few moments to remember what had happened. I decided it must have been a dream, but what was I doing lying on the couch and not in bed? Throwing back the rug that was covering me, I saw I was still naked. I looked around for my nightie and saw it in a crumpled mess on the floor.

I stood on shaky legs. The fire was still burning; someone or something had thrown more logs on to keep me warm. Grabbing the rug, I wrapped it around my naked body. As I walked my pussy lips rubbed together, swollen from so much activity. I was confused. Last night couldn't have been a dream, but what else could it have been?

I didn't believe in ghosts, never have. I checked all the windows and doors. Everything was still locked as I'd left it. It would have been impossible for someone to have entered the cabin unbeknown to me, yet someone must have and I had the bruises to prove it.

I ran the bath and lowered my aching body into it.

Lying back in the warmth I went over in my mind all that had happened. Mary! No one else knew where we used to hide the strap-on when we were here. It had to have been her.

I sat up quickly, water spilling over the edges to slop onto the floor. It must have been her coming to me with others, giving me what we'd always dreamed of. An orgy! Was it possible? Really possible?

Grabbing a towel I hurried over to my typewriter. There, placed neatly on the table was my final chapter. I picked up the first page and began to read. An hour later I finished. It was brilliant, the sex scenes so real, so vivid.

Who had written these words? Could I use them? Where they mine? I debated with myself whether this was plagiarism. Who had I plagiarized? Who would sue me? A dead person!

As I sat there shivering in my wet towel I decided to write a new novel. A sequel to my last. I decided to call it, *My Unknown Lover*. I threw on my robe, wrapping it tightly around my nakedness and began to tap at the keys.

Many hours later, I discovered that I'd written better than I ever had before. Starving for food, certainly not for inspiration, I quickly ate a rushed dinner, grabbed another bottle of wine, and continued on with my writing.

Needing to use the bathroom, I stopped dead when I saw what was in there. On the bathroom mirror, smeared with my lipstick, were words I thought I'd never see again.

I'll always love you...Mary.

Later that night, nude, I lay back on the couch, hoping Mary would return, to give me new stimulus for inspiration.

ABOUT THE CONTRIBUTORS

CHERYL B's work has appeared in dozens of print and online publications, including *BLOOM, Small Spiral Notebook*, and *The Guardian*. She has received a fellowship from the New York Foundation for the Arts and has been a resident at the Virginia Center for the Creative Arts. She lives in Brooklyn and online at www.cherylb.com.

RASHELLE BROWN's most recent work has appeared in *The Lesbian News Magazine* and *Ultimate Undies: Erotic Stories about Underwear and Lingerie*. She is currently working on her first novel, while working full-time, attending graduate school, and undertaking a major renovation to her home. She needs a cruise like the one in her story very badly.

The various scribblings of author **TENILLE BROWN** are featured online and in several print anthologies, including *Amazons*; *Glamour Girls*; *Ultimate Undies*; *Sexiest Soles*; *Caught Looking*; and *African-American Women Authors: An A to Z Guide.* Visit her at www.tenillebrown.com.

RACHEL KRAMER BUSSEL (www.rachelkramerbussel. com) has edited or co-edited nine erotic anthologies, including the Lambda Literary Award finalist *Up All Night*, *First-Timers: True Stories of Lesbian Awakening*; *Glamour Girls: Femme/Femme Erotica*; *Ultimate Undies*, *Sexiest Soles*, *Secret Slaves: Erotic Stories of Bondage*; *Naughty Spanking Stories from A to Z, 1 and 2*; and *Caught Looking: Erotic Tales of Voyeurs and Exhibitionists.* She serves as senior editor at *Penthouse Variations*, writes the Lusty Lady column for the *Village Voice*, hosts the In the Flesh Erotic Reading Series, and contributes to Bust, Gothamist, Mediabistro, *The New York Post*, and other publications. When she's not writing smut, she's blogging about cupcakes and going to comedy shows.

CHERI CRYSTAL is a health care professional by day and a writer of lesbian erotica and romance by night. She has stories in *Lessons in Love: Erotic Interludes 3*, edited by Radclyffe and Stacia Seaman (May 2006); *After Midnight*,

True Lesbian Erotic Confessions (ed. Chelsea James; July 2006), and is currently working on a romance novel.

ANDREA DALE's stories have appeared in *Ultimate Undies*, The MILF Anthology, *Best Lesbian Erotica 2005*, and Fishnetmag.com, among others. With coauthors, she has written *A Little Night Music* as Sarah Dale (Cheek Books) and *Cat Scratch Fever* as Sophie Mouette (Black Lace Books). Visit her at www.cyvarwydd.com.

ALISON DUBOIS has had quite a few stories published in various Alyson anthologies, among them, *Awakening the Virgin; Up All Night; Early Embraces III*; and *Show and Tell*. She is also the author of the newly released book, *She Kissed Me*, a pictorial odyssey depicting what kissing means to lesbians and the lesbian community. Ms. Dubois is currently touring to promote the book. For more information on the book and where she is touring, please visit her Web site: shekissedme.citymaker.com.

AUNT FANNY stories appear in Bold Strokes Books's *Extreme Passions* and Lammy-winning *Stolen Moments*, as well as *Ultimate Lesbian Erotica 2006* and *2007* by Alyson Books; Cleis Press's *Best Lesbian Romance 2007*; and Bella Books's *Wild Nights: True Lesbian Sex Stories*. Contact her at auntfannystories@yahoo.com.

KRISTIE HELMS is the author of *Dish It Up Baby* (Firebrand Books), a 2004 Lambda Literary Award finalist. Her work has appeared in *Utne, The New York Press*,

Genre, I Do/I Don't: Queers on Marriage; Pinned Down by Pronouns; and *Ultimate Undies: Erotic Stories About Lingerie and Underwear.* www.dishitupbaby.com.

Erotic writer **EVA HORE**, from Australia, has been widely published throughout the United Kingdom, United States, and Europe. Her work has appeared in anthologies, magazines, and on the Web.

YURI is a twenty-five-year-old bisexual woman who recently graduated with a B.A. in humanities from the University of Louisville. This will hopefully be the first of many publications during her writing career. She is currently taking a year off from school to pursue her dream.

JESI O'CONNELL's erotica has been published in *Back to Basics: A Butch/Femme Anthology; My Lover, My Friend: True-life Stories of Lesbian Romance Between Friends; Wet: True Lesbian Sex Stories;* and *Awakening the Virgin: Real-Life Encounters of Lesbians & Virgins.* She lives in the red rock country of southern Utah.

SHANEL ODUM is a Brooklyn-based scribe and universal lover of words. The magazine editor by day, bartender by night, confesses that she conducted lots of research during her first attempt at erotic storytelling.

TRICIA OWENS is the owner and writer of Juxta-poseFantasy.com, a professional gay fiction site. She has been writing gay fiction since 2002 and hopes to expand the market and encourage new writers through her various business projects. She may be reached at tricia@juxtaposefantasy.com.

TERESA NOELLE ROBERTS writes erotica, poetry, romance, and speculative fiction. Her erotica has appeared in *Best Women's Erotica 2004, 2005,* and *2007*; FishNetMag; and many other publications. She is also one-half of the erotica-writing duo Sophie Mouette, whose novel *Cat Scratch Fever* was released in 2006 by Black Lace Books. She cannot fix anything.

LIEZL SARTO is a freelance writer residing in Long Beach, California. Painting, drawing, and sleeping (all in the nude) are just a few of her favorite pastimes. Her aptitude for design has recently inspired her to pursue the dream of being an architect. Liezl can be contacted at liezl_sarto@yahoo.com.

DIANE THIBAULT is a queer writer and translator who lives in Toronto, Canada. She enjoys pushing the boundaries of lesbian adventure in her writing and in her life. Her work has appeared in *S.M.U.T. Magazine, Hot Lesbian Erotica 2005,* and *Sexiest Soles: Erotic Stories About Feet and Shoes.*

JULES TORTI has been creating fantasies in her mind for other women in their pants for a decade. Her slippery stories have appeared in *Hot & Bothered 1, 2,* and *3; Awakening the Virgin; Beginnings; Early Embraces*

2; and *The Mammoth Book of Erotica*. She lives on the west coast of Canada with her muse and her dog, and is tapping out a clit lit novel in between her real life as a massage therapist.

RAKELLE VALENCIA co-edited Lambda Literary Award-finalist *Rode Hard, Put Away Wet*; *Hard Road, Easy Riding*; and *Lipstick on Her Collar* with Sacchi Green and *Drag Kings: Tales of Lesbian Erotica* with Am M. Evans. Rakelle has been published in *Blood Sisters*; *Red Hot Erotica*; *Ultimate Lesbian Erotica 2006*; *The Good Parts: Pure Lesbian Erotica*; *Best Lesbian Love Stories 2005*; *Hot Lesbian Erotica 2005*; *Ultimate Lesbian Erotica 2005*; *Best Bondage Erotica 2*; *Best of Best Lesbian Erotica 2*; *Best Lesbian Erotica 2005*; *Naughty Spanking Stories from A to Z*; *Best Lesbian Erotica 2004*; *On Our Backs: The Best Erotic Fiction Vol. 2*; and *On Our Backs*. Rakelle is a 2006 semifinalist in the Project: Queer Lit Contest.

EVA VANDETUIN, a religious studies graduate student, sees sex and spirituality as being closely intertwined. She has been published in *Clean Sheets*, *The Dominant's View*, and *Lessons in Love: Erotic Interludes 3*.

M. J. WILLIAMZ lives in Portland, Oregon, where inspiration for writing erotica abounds. Her erotic short stories have appeared in *The Good Parts*; *Back 2 Basics*; *The Perfect Valentine*; and *Blood Sisters*. She's currently putting the finishing touches on her novel, *Mystic Sage*, which she hopes to have published soon.

KRISTINA WRIGHT's erotic fiction has appeared in more than thirty anthologies, including two previous editions of *Ultimate Lesbian Erotica*; *The Mammoth Book of Best New Erotica, Volumes 5* and *6*; *Best Women's Erotica 2000* and *2007*; and four editions of *Best Lesbian Erotica*. In addition to being a full-time writer, Kristina is pursuing a graduate degree in humanities. For more information about her life, writing, and academic pursuits, visit her at www.kristinawright.com.

ROXANNE YORK likes to seduce straight girls using lipstick, heels, and a killer smile. She writes dirty stories when she's inspired, and can otherwise be found knitting, people watching, and dyeing her hair.